CROSSCOURT WINNER

To Mom, who taught me how to take risks without worrying about failure and how to look for answers to the really Big Questions.

"For God did not give us a spirit of timidity, but a spirit of power and love and self-control" (2 Timothy 1:7).

Thank you for teaching me how to walk without fear and think on my own.

CROSSCOURT WINNER

**JEFFREY
ARCHER
NESBIT**

VICTOR BOOKS

A DIVISION OF SCRIPTURE PRESS PUBLICATIONS INC.
USA CANADA ENGLAND

THE CAPITAL CREW SERIES
Crosscourt Winner
The Lost Canoe
The Reluctant Runaway
Struggle with Silence

Cover illustration by Kathy Kulin-Sandel

Library of Congress Cataloging-in-Publication Data:
Nesbit, Jeffrey Asher.
    Crosscourt winner / by Jeffrey Asher Nesbit.
        p.   cm.   — (The Capital crew)
    Summary: After his father deserts the family, Cally moves with his
    mother and six siblings to the Washington, D.C., area, where he
    develops his tennis skills, skirmishes with an athletic rival, and
    accepts Christ into his life.
    ISBN 0-89693-129-3
    [1. Moving, Household—Fiction. 2. Tennis—Fiction. 3. Family
    life—Fiction. 4. Christian life—Fiction.]   I. Title.   II. Series.
    PZ7.N4378Cr   1991
    [Fic]—dc20   90-27618
                                                                        CIP
                                                                         AC

1 2 3 4 5 6 7 8 9 10 Printing/Year 95 94 93 92 91

VICTOR BOOKS
A division of SP Publications, Inc.
Wheaton, Illinois 60187

Prologue

So here I am, after all.

"Here" is Aunt Tildy's, in Indianapolis, Indiana, with her five kids, right after Christmas, waiting for the National Indoor Tennis Championship to begin.

I've super-glued the sole of my right Brooks tennis shoe for the very last, I repeat, very last time. My mother has double-stitched the seat of my only pair of white shorts, just to make sure.

My socks are clean, for a change, and Aunt Tildy even pressed my white, 100 percent cotton shirt. All is in order. The world is exactly as it should be.

Well, not exactly as it should be, but it'll do for a start. I can hardly even hear Timmy crying in the room at the back of the house. Karen's eternal silence seems like heaven to my weary, battered soul. Jana has cooled her jets at last.

John is still John. All things considered, though, as usual, I don't have a clue what his cluttered, photographic mind is up to at the moment.

Susan, bless her ever-loving heart, gave up one of her favorite shows to clean the tar off my other Brooks. I protested. I really did. She just wouldn't listen.

And Chris, well, Chris has simply disappeared. I know he's taking this whole thing much, much too seriously. It will all vanish in a big puff of smoke. I know it. But just try convincing him of that all-too-obvious reality.

You see, while I'm here at Aunt Tildy's, everyone

else is at the Hilton or the Marriott downtown, where the price of a room for one night would pay for our family's meals for the next week.

They're trying to figure out how they can possibly carry all eight or nine of their Donnay graphites in one bag. I'm wondering if my cat gut can hold out through just one more tournament.

OK, OK, maybe I'm exaggerating just a little. They only have four or five rackets and maybe they're slumming at Burger King. But it still adds up to the same thing. I don't have a prayer. Not a one.

Listen to me, God, I'm happy right now. I really am. You've done more than I ever thought was possible. I didn't believe her at first, but I believe Mom now when she tells me about all those promises in the Bible. You know, like what Jesus said: "Seek, and you will find." I asked You for this chance, just to get this far, and You've delivered.

Really and truly, I don't care all that much if I don't get a shot at Evan Grant, if I never see his mug across the net. It won't matter much if I don't get a crack at some of those rich kids who are seeded at the top of the tournament. Just see me through the qualifying . . .

Oh, who am I kidding? I'd like nothing better than to take every last one of them on. It won't happen, of course. Chris can talk himself blue in the face. It won't happen. I'm just not in their league.

Maybe I should back up a little, like, how did I get here in the first place, why am I cowering in fear in my aunt's house and who is this motley crew joining me on my sojourn through fantasyland?

The last part's easy. The crew is my family. They're my brothers and sisters, for better or worse, and I'm their oldest brother, whether they like it or not. As for the rest of it, well. . . .

My father means nothing to me. There's no way around it. Believe me, I've tried. I've pleaded his case in my mind so many times . . .

If my father is out there somewhere in the great dark of the night, making his way merrily, I hope someone tells him I'm here. Remembering. Tell him I go to sleep at night with my hands clenched in rage. . . .

You know, I don't care that he lost his job and couldn't find it again. As if that had anything at all to do with our family.

My father's first job out of high school was at Cyclops Steel, down in the valley in Birmingham, Alabama, the heart of the old, deep South. It was a good job. It paid well. By the time Susan was born, he was making about twenty bucks an hour, with more than a decade of seniority.

And then the American steel industry collapsed. Korea, Japan, Brazil, Venezuela, Argentina . . . they all started making steel better than we could. They made it cheaper, sold it cheaper. They pushed our boys right off the map and there wasn't a thing we could do about it.

I mean, how do you hold onto your job, my father complained endlessly, when the Koreans are working twelve-hour days for two bucks an hour. How? What can you do when they discover that a robot can pour molten steel better than you can, that a robot never gets tired or makes a mistake? How do you fight it?

You can't.

My father raged, and my mother prayed. Silently, with a kind of firm, quiet insistence that God make it all right again with our family. With my father's world crumbling, it was my mother and her rock-solid faith that kept our family from pulling apart at the seams.

It was funny, but you could see the fear take my father over. He'd come home after a shift with that look, the one I'd come to recognize. The layoff look. When they were starting to send guys home with six or seven years experience, that's when he started to get a little crazy.

It was about then that he went on this American stuff. American this, American that. We had to have Budweiser in the fridge. He drove a Ford truck and my mother drove the kids around in a Chevy station wagon.

The TV was a Magnavox, not a Sony. The blender was made in Hoboken, New Jersey, not Taiwan. Every single piece of furniture came from somewhere in North Carolina. Our clothes came from South Carolina.

It happened, finally. My father went on an all-night drunk and by the time he straggled in at the crack of dawn, we'd all heard that they'd finally decided to close the mill for good.

Somehow, we managed to get by. We kept our house on the mountain. That's where all the other nice houses are, overlooking the city.

When the unemployment and the trade adjustment payments ran out, my father stopped going to the union hall. Oh, he still went out with his friends just about every night. But I think he'd given up.

I don't know when he met *her*. Maybe it was in a bar somewhere some night. Maybe it was at the bowling alley, or on the bus, or at the pool hall. It doesn't matter, I guess.

All that really matters is that he met her. And she told him what a wonderful, kind, loving person he was. That's what he wanted to hear. Not from my mother — who'd always told him that, even before they got married — but from *her*. He needed to hear it. His old life was over. He wanted a new one.

So he left a note. A lousy, miserable note. "I'm sorry," he said. "I'll send money when I get back on my feet. I just couldn't take it anymore. I was losing my mind. I was . . ."

Me, me, me. Was that all he was thinking about when he left?

Well, as far as I'm concerned, I can live without you, Father. Hit the road and stay there. We'll survive without you. No, we'll do better than that. We'll succeed. God, I know Mom always says that it isn't our place to judge others, even when it seems they're doing horrible, terrible things. But . . .

My mother put the house up for sale after he left. It sold right away because she priced it way below what it was worth. We don't need such an expensive house, she told me. Not to mention the memories.

We loaded all the furniture on a rented truck one weekend. I said good-bye to a few friends. And we left town. No forwarding address, no ties to the past. If he could start a new life, then we could too.

That's really where this story starts. The only reason I even mentioned my father at all is because, well, he started it all. We'd probably still be in Birmingham if he hadn't gone over the edge.

"When do we get there, Mommy? When, huh?" Susan was squished between us on the seat of the truck, peering brightly over the dashboard at the Appalachian Mountains on our left.

There were five of us in the seat. I had one hand draped over Timmy—who'd just turned two months old—in his car seat. John's head rested on my shoulder. Susan was sitting next to my mother, leaning against her as she drove in her ever-cautious manner. She was driving especially carefully because we were towing our old Chevy station wagon behind us.

"Soon," my mother said with a weary sigh.

"You said that already," Susan pouted. " 'Bout a hundred years ago."

"All right, then we have hours and hours to go. We'll be there tomorrow," she said with a straight face.

"Nooooooooh!" Susan wailed, jostling my mother's arm as she began to pound on the dash. "That's not true . . ."

"You can't have it both ways, Susan," my mother said reasonably. "We'll either be there soon, or we'll be there tomorrow. Take your pick."

Susan scrunched up her face angrily. I tried not to laugh. She took everything so seriously. "All right," she said finally. "Then you have to tell me. Just where is this Washington place? Is it far from home?"

"Yes, very far," my mother answered. "You've been there before—when you were three."

"I don't remember. Is it a nice place?"

"*I* think so. Your uncle says it is."

"Are we staying with Uncle Teddy?"

"For a bit. Until I can find a job."

"When will that be? How long? Will you be away when I come home from school?"

My mother closed her eyes, but only for the briefest moment. Her eyes were riveted on the road ahead as she spoke. "Susan, dear. I can't answer those questions just yet. You know that. We've talked about this and talked about it. . . ."

I reached out and put a hand on Susan's shoulder. "Somebody'll be there, kid. Don't worry."

"Will I like the school?" she asked me.

My mother started to shake her head, so I cut her off before she could answer. "Yes, you'll like it," I said. "How many times have I told you that, huh? Do you have a brain or what?"

I reached behind her head and tugged on her red ponytail gently. Susan giggled. " 'Course I have a brain," she said. "Better'n yours."

Which was true. Susan's smart as a whip. So is John, but for a different reason.

I rubbed one eye as I kept the other on the highway. Both my eyes were killing me. "Piece o' cake," I'd told my mother when she asked me to watch the road with her as she drove. Just in case, she said. She hadn't told me how tough it is to keep your eyes glued to the road, though.

I glanced at the clock and sighed softly. It was five minutes past when I should have checked on my brother and sisters in the back. I reached over my shoulder and gave the back wall of the cab three solid raps.

Chris rapped back almost immediately. "You're late, turkey!" I heard a muffled voice shout. I smiled. That was just like Chris to sit there and wait for me to mess up.

Chris, Karen, and Jana had volunteered to ride with the furniture in the back. We'd arranged it so that I'd knock on the cab every half hour to make sure everybody was all right. If I didn't get an answer, then Mom stopped the truck to see what had happened.

The three of them are just about as different as three kids could be. Karen and Jana are twins and a year younger than me—they're twelve—but they're not identical so they don't really act like twins.

Karen's got really short brown hair. She always has this stern look on her face, like she knows she has a math final coming up in an hour. She does almost as much around the house as my mother does. Maybe more, I don't know.

Karen does most of the cooking, too. She's a great cook. She likes to make exotic stuff. It always gave my father a kick. Personally, I'd just as soon go down to Mac's for a few cheeseburgers. I'd never say it out loud, of course. Karen would take my head off.

Jana is . . . how do I describe it? Waiting to get into trouble? Naive, innocent, carefree, oblivious to what she does to guys when she walks into a room? I guess those all fit.

Jana has long, rich, lustrous black hair. She has a face that makes your heart melt. She also has the mind of a little girl, or so she pretends. Still, if this makes sense, she sure does seem a lot older than twelve. . . .

Jana barely makes it through school each year. She

spends more time brushing her hair at night than she does looking at school books. If it took her any longer to pick out a wardrobe in the morning, they'd have to cancel classes.

But for some strange, bizarre, incredible reason, Karen and Jana are about as tight as two sisters can be. I've heard them whispering secretively to each other until all hours of the night.

They talk about everything under the sun. The two of them go almost everywhere together—shopping, roller-skating, you name it. It's a good thing too. I'm pretty sure Karen keeps Jana out of trouble.

And Chris? Well, Chris is one of a kind. Two years younger than me, with black hair like Jana's that constantly falls in his eyes, he always has an answer for everything. The way he looks at the world is downright unusual.

Not only does he have an answer for everything, Chris never thinks anything is bad. The wind was created to keep him cool in the summertime, not push in his face as he tries to bike up a hill. Grass isn't there in your front yard to be mowed, it's there to cushion your fall during a pickup football game.

In Chris' world, you don't climb stairs, you run up them as fast as you can to get to the top. You don't grumble about homework, you thank your lucky stars that the teacher only assigned 10 pages, not 20, and that you can still finish in time for the movie on television.

And your father doesn't abandon seven kids and a mother who would climb Mt. Everest to make their life better. No, your father gives you a chance to go to a faraway land where mysterious adventures are waiting just around the corner...

Like I said, Chris is one of a kind. There's never

been anyone like him, I don't think. Probably never will be. At least, I hope not. You can take that kind of boundless hope, good will, and enthusiasm for just so long.

John, four years younger than me, is in a class by himself as well. We didn't know about his gift until one day, when he was about five or six, he started rattling off weird facts. Calippus was a Greek astronomer, he told us. A caliver is a gun. Calixtus was a pope.

My mother discovered the encyclopedia volume in the den, where John had left it. It was open to a page—Calippus to Calixtus—and my mother realized instantly that her third son was blessed with a photographic memory. Or cursed with one.

Because, you see, John remembers everything. He has almost total recall. He still hasn't figured out how to put it all in some kind of order, however, which can make for a very confusing conversation.

Now, Susan is a paper doll, a cutout kid if I've ever seen one. She's seven, two years younger than John, and a regular little angel. We have no idea where her red hair came from. It hasn't been around for at least two generations.

She's always asking questions, about everything under the sun, and always sticking her nose where it shouldn't be. Which is usually in my business. She's like my shadow when I'm around the house.

If I pick out a book in the den, she will too. If I take my racket out to bang a ball against the back wall, she grabs another tennis ball and joins me, throwing it off the wall and asking a question on every other bounce.

I don't know why Timmy came along, exactly. He just sort of arrived on our doorstep one afternoon. Not really, of course. But it was unexpected.

I mean, it had been seven years since Susan was born. And my mother had always joked so much about when we were all babies—you know, changing the diapers, staying up at night, yanking us out of theaters when we started to bawl.

So it was kind of a shock the day she announced that we were all going to have another little brother or sister. My father sure didn't look happy at the time. He could feel the ax at the back of his neck already and the prospect of another mouth to feed made him look like he was sick to his stomach.

I heard him first talking about it in the bathroom. They didn't think anyone was around. But I was half in the bedroom when I heard my father start to raise his voice.

"I can't believe you did this to me," he said in an angry, forced whisper. "You wanted this kid. You thought it would help. Well, you're wrong. It'll just make it worse."

"No, you're wrong. This is a blessing from God. You'll see. Everything will work out—"

"Oh, don't give me that nonsense about God making everything work out," he half-shouted. "It won't, which is why you're going to the doctor. Tomorrow. We can't afford another kid. Not now. You're gonna have it fixed. You're too old anyway."

That's when I heard my mother gasp. It's also when I decided to march into the room like I'd planned to before. Only now I had to pretend I'd never heard a thing . . .

Timmy was born eight months later. I never heard them talk about it again. I think they knew that I'd been listening. I can't be sure.

Anyway, that's the whole family, for better or

worse. They're all good kids, every last one of them. I think Timmy will be the most special of all, if only because he'll always be living proof that my father lost his war against our family.

We pulled into Fairfax County, just outside Washington, D.C., about an hour after dinnertime. The family hadn't been to see Uncle Teddy in almost four years. Now, at least for awhile, this was our new home.

My uncle is a trip. I think he works for the CIA. I don't really know, because he never tells us what he does for a living. All I know is that he lives in a nice house, drives a nice car, and smiles a lot.

The last time we came for a visit, he gave me my first tennis lesson. He took me to an indoor club he belongs to, paid to use a ball machine for a half hour and made me hit forehands down the line the entire time.

I had blisters like you wouldn't believe the next day, but I didn't really mind. Because my uncle had taught me something that I would remember for a long time to come. You have to practice something—even something you love dearly—over and over until you've mastered it. The principle works with almost anything.

My Uncle Teddy also told me four years ago that I was a natural. A tennis player with all the right moves. I didn't believe him, of course. My uncle, for reasons of his own, likes to exaggerate sometimes.

But it did get me to thinking. I did like the feel of a racket in my hand. The first time I shook hands with one, I felt a little tingle run up my forearm.

The first time I tossed the ball high in the air and smashed a serve, I hardly even cared that it caromed off the fence. The power and speed of it, the whip at the end, that's what amazed me.

So that summer, after visiting my uncle, I went to the closest public park in Birmingham, signed up for the summer league, and played in a few tournaments.

I've played tennis every summer since, mostly for the fun of it. I was smart enough to realize early on that tennis is a rich man's game, so I never took it seriously.

Oh, I won a few park tournaments, collected a few dinky trophies and a plaque or two. But it was all just for fun. Just something to pass the time of day in the heat of summer.

Somewhere in the ozone layers of my soul, I suppose I wondered what it would be like to play in the real tournaments around the country, to play with some of the hotshot, rich kids whose parents have pushed tennis on them since they were old enough to walk.

I've read all the tennis magazines. I've watched all the pro tournaments and I once sat through the Birmingham Open from start to finish on the pro circuit. But, trust me, I would never actually dream about taking it too seriously. It just isn't reasonable.

You see, it takes money to play real tennis. Lots of money. Tennis rackets cost a pile of money. So do shoes and sweats and wardrobes. And to play in the really big, high-class tournaments, you gotta have money to travel with.

All of which definitely disqualifies me. Even if I am a natural. Even if I can hit a crosscourt backhand that would knock the racket out of your hand.

* * * * *

"Why, Carl Lee James, how you've grown!" exclaimed my aunt—my other aunt, Uncle Teddy's wife, Francis.

"C'mon, Aunt Franny, you know my name," I said with a frown.

"Now, now, young man, we both know Cally is hardly a proper name for a young boy," my aunt said, putting on her sternest face.

"He likes the name Cally," my mother said softly, coming to my rescue.

You see, I hate the name I was born with. Carl sort of sounds like you've got something in your throat. As luck would have it, though, Karen had never been able to say my name when we were young. She tried to say "Carl Lee" and it came out "Cally." Which is now my name. Forever and ever.

"Well, it's still no name for a proper young man," my aunt grumbled.

Fortune smiled on me then though, as the rest of the family piled into the house. As always, Timmy almost immediately became the star attraction, the center of attention.

I helped Chris and John unpack the stuff from the rental truck that we'd need. Just clothes, mostly. We were staying at my uncle's until my mother could find a job, which might be never.

My mother hadn't had a job since I was born. In fact, she'd only finished three years of college when our dear father made her quit school. He, of course, never went to college. No need to, he always said. A real man worked with his hands and earned a living.

Which meant, of course, that my mother had absolutely nothing at all in the world to fall back on. Housework, raising seven wonderful kids, and serving a rotten husband on bended knee are hardly market-able skills. That last one, maybe, but it isn't the kind of thing you put in a job application.

"Don't you worry about a thing, Marilynn," Uncle Teddy told my mother that night after dinner. I could just barely hear the conversation from the kitchen. I'd volunteered to do the dishes, something I do about once in a blue moon.

"And how am I supposed to manage that?" my mother said, sighing. "Eight mouths to feed. Not much in the bank . . ."

"What about the house?" my uncle asked.

"The bottom dropped right out of the housing mar-ket in Birmingham," my mother said. "I pretty much got our down payment back and a little bit more. That's about it."

My uncle whistled. "And that won't go far."

"I figure it'll last about six months, at best," said my mother, the budgetmaker. "Maybe more, if we can find a cheap house to rent."

I could hear Uncle Teddy lean back in his chair. "I'll tell you something, Marilynn. You might think about looking for a job in another part of the country. The standard of living here . . ."

"I know," my mother said sharply. "It's high. I've already priced homes here. They're absolutely absurd. But the school system, that's what I care about."

"And it's one of the best in the country, no question about it," Aunt Franny said. I could just see her nod-ding her head sagely.

"That it is," my uncle agreed. "Top rate."

"Which is why I want to see if we can make a go of it here," my mother said. "It's worth the risk."

"Well, you can rest easy about Timmy," said Aunt Franny, bless her soul. "You know that I'm tickled pink at the thought of watching him during the day."

There was a long silence. "You know I appreciate it, Franny. I really do," my mother said slowly. "I don't especially like it, but it's not like I have a choice. . . ."

"Now, now," my aunt clucked. "Never you mind about that worrying. Timmy will be just fine. You go out and find yourself the best job you can."

"And don't sell yourself short, Marilynn," my uncle warned her. "You have good qualities you're not even aware of yet."

"But Teddy," my mother pleaded, "I haven't had a job in nearly twenty years, and the last one was waiting tables in a diner."

"Marilynn," my aunt said softly. "You know the Lord will provide. You know He will. It'll just take a little, tiny bit of faith right now."

"Franny's right. And I meant what I said before," my uncle said firmly. "You may have to get your foot in the door somewhere, but you have a first-rate mind."

"I can take on a paper route, Mom," I called out from the kitchen, as I dried off the last plate.

"Cally, come in here," my mother said loudly after a slight pause. I obeyed, reluctantly.

I tried to head her off at the pass. "Now, Mom, I know—"

"Hush," she said. "Sit and listen to me. You are not getting up at the crack of dawn just to make money from a paper route, and that's that. You need the sleep right now. Without that, you won't do well in school."

"But Mom," I pleaded, "what if we need the money? I can help, some."

"Cally, Cally," she sighed. "How many times are we going to have this conversation?"

"Until you say yes," I said, trying not to smile.

"Which isn't likely to happen anytime soon," my mother said, her eyes blazing.

"But what if I can find a route that I can throw in an hour? That's not much. Just an hour," I said. Then I suddenly switched directions. "And anyway, you didn't say anything about the job I had this summer with the parks system in Birmingham—"

"That was different and you know it," she said sharply. "That wasn't a job. Teaching tennis to little kids is fine for the summer. A paper route during the school year is entirely something else again."

My uncle cleared his throat. We all looked at him. When he does that, it usually means he wants to stick his big nose where it has no right to be.

"Marilynn," he said gently, "what if I could find something for Cally right after school, something where he could earn a little pocket change and have some fun too?"

"Such as?" my mother said skeptically.

"Well, I know for a fact that the pro at the indoor tennis club we belong to needs a little bit of help," he said hesitantly. "I'm sure I can pull a few strings."

"That'd be great!" I almost shouted. "That would be so tough."

"Now, hold on," my uncle cautioned. "You'd get a first-hand look at something you've always shown a keen interest in. You'd get a lot of playing time in for free and maybe even teach a little—"

"Holy cow!" I said.

". . . but you'd also have to pick up after the members and generally keep your big mouth shut," he continued, completely ignoring my outburst. "You would undoubtedly do your share of the scut work."

"So what?" I shrugged. "I can handle it. Just as long as they let me out on the courts in my free time."

"I don't see a problem with that," my uncle said.

"Hold on," said the central figure in this game. "I'm not so sure I like where this is going. Not a bit."

"Oh, Mom, it's a great opportunity," I said, trying to sound as reasonable as I possibly could. "I may never get a chance to do something like this ever again."

"And your studying? What do you intend to do about that?" she demanded.

"I'll make the time," I promised. "Don't worry."

"He'll have a chance to study all he wants at the club, while he's watching the sign-in desk," my uncle offered.

"See?" I said triumphantly. "No problem. It'll work out just great."

"I don't know," my mother said hesitantly. "I still don't like it."

"But you'll say yes, won't you?" I said quickly, seizing the opening she'd provided. "At least until we see if it's working or not?"

She stared at me for a long time, longer than she usually does when she's deciding the fate of the known universe. "All right," she said finally. "Two months. We'll give it two months and then take another look at it. OK by you?"

"Yeah, sure," I said, barely able to contain my excitement.

It was all I could do to keep from hopping all over the living room like a Mexican jumping bean.

*   *   *   *   *

I don't know how he did it, but then I never know how Uncle Teddy does anything. He's so mysterious about everything.

I got the job at the Royal Racquet Club and began some informal lessons with the pro there, Steve Walker.

My mother bought a new pair of shoes at the end of the summer.

Now, normally, that sort of thing doesn't draw attention to it. Oh sure, occasionally it does. When I was seven, I set the world record. I went through twenty-three pairs of sneakers in a summer.

How did I manage that? Easy. I ran nonstop from the moment I woke up until I came to a screeching halt at sundown, that's how. Try skidding to a stop in an alley hundreds of times during the course of a summer and see how many sneakers you wear out.

But my mother went through a pair of brand-new brown leather shoes in just two weeks. This is the same mother who still owns dresses she wore in the fifth grade and coats that went out of style twenty years ago.

You see, nobody would give her a job. Nobody would even listen to her. And to save money—because parking a car in Washington, D.C. is horribly expensive—she walked everywhere. She'd walk from one job interview to the next, even if they were a mile or so apart.

"I can't afford the cabs in this town," she told me.

It's just not fair, I thought that night. *Why won't anybody listen to her? Why will no one give her the time of day? Explain that to me. My mother has some*

*great qualities. So why are they ignoring her? Listen,
God, if You're really as powerful as my mom says You
are, then why won't anyone help her? Why?*

Uncle Teddy told her not to worry, of course. He
always tells everyone not to worry. "Everything will
turn out right in the end," he says. "Just wait and
see."

One night, he said, "Marilynn, I'll say it one more
time. Don't worry. There's a job out there with your
name on it. Trust me."

"But the kids have to start school soon," she pleaded. "Where do I send them? And I can't just stay here
indefinitely, eating you out of house and home . . ."

That's when Uncle Teddy took her aside. He does
that sometimes too. He drapes a big arm around your
shoulders, leans real close and tells you he doesn't
want any boo-hoos in his house. Face the world. Don't
fear it. And don't cry about what you can't change.

"Marilynn, what's that passage from the Bible
you're so fond of quoting?" Uncle Teddy said, kidding
her a little.

My mother sighed. "Even sparrows don't fall to the
ground unless it's God's will, and I'm worth more than
a sparrow," she said.

"Well?"

"OK, OK," my mother said. "But my feet still hurt
from all this walking."

My mother really never stopped worrying, of course.
But she did stop looking like the world was about to
end every time we sat down to dinner. She stopped
counting the potatoes on all our plates, trying to figure
how much money she was costing Uncle Teddy each
day we spent at his house. And she also found out
which schools we were supposed to go to.

"Not much choice, really," Uncle Teddy said about

my school. "Roosevelt's the closest. And it's pretty good. It has a decent reputation." He gave me a wink.

I knew what that meant. There was one other reason why Roosevelt was a good school. Roosevelt, he told me later, has the best tennis team in the area. Very few junior high schools have tennis teams, but Roosevelt's one of them.

"Went to the state championships last year," he said when my mother wasn't around. "And everybody's returning this year, including this hotshot twelve-year-old, Evan Grant, who was allowed to play on the team last year even though he wasn't in junior high yet. You see, Grant's ranked nationally—"

"Ranked? Nationally?" I gasped.

"Yep," Uncle Teddy said. "Grant made it to the quarterfinals of the 12-and-under during the U.S. Open last year."

My head was spinning. There was someone that good in the area, who was going to Roosevelt? And I'd have to go up against him?

"But I won't have a chance of making the team, not against the ninth-graders," I protested.

"You'll make it. Trust me," he said confidently. "I've seen them play. And you're better, even if you are two years younger than some of them."

Me, I wasn't so sure. Uncle Teddy can pull a lot of strings, but this wasn't one of them. I'd have to make the team on my own. And they'd probably blow my doors off.

I saw Evan Grant too many times on the first day of school—during class, afterwards, when his mother picked him up in their Cadillac, and then again that night at the tennis club, where he was an exclusive junior member.

Exclusive junior members carry a whopping amount of clout at the club. They're allowed to demand just about anything they want. Within reason. And Evan Grant makes full use of those privileges.

The snack bar, I discovered, delivers an occasional chocolate milkshake to him while he's out on the courts. That, as I'm sure you can imagine, is strictly forbidden at the club. But Evan gets away with it.

Evan's father, you see, is Ethan Grant. Look him up in the *Who's Who.* You'll discover that he is a direct descendant of one of our past presidents, supposedly a drunk of a general who accidentally wound up in the White House.

When someone at school told me this about Evan Grant, I couldn't help but laugh. Our family, through my father, can thank its existence to a crook—Jesse James. We were the new James Gang, direct descendants of one of the James boys. We certainly inherited no money, only an infamous legacy from a crummy outlaw.

Ethan Grant, meanwhile, benefited nicely from the

fact that one of his forebears had been a United States President. Presidents tend to amass fortunes, whether they want to or not. Ancestors inherit them, whether they are worthy of them or not. I had no idea whether Ethan Grant was worthy or not. All I knew was that his son was one of the best tennis players I'd ever seen. And a jerk.

It was my first class. I'd quickly grabbed the first empty seat. That's when I heard it.

"What a backwater hick," a voice whispered loud enough so I could hear. I glanced around to see where the voice had come from. I was met by a haughty stare two rows over.

The guy had perfectly combed, sandy blond hair, an unblemished face, a pert little nose, thin lips, narrow cheeks, and slender shoulders. He had a fairly decent build to him, though. Gangly and wiry, sort of.

At this particular moment, he was staring at me with the most conceited grin I'd ever seen. He'd obviously been the author of the statement, because a few of his friends were chuckling around him, trying to avoid my glance.

I looked hard at the kid, weighing in my mind whether I wanted to clean his clock after class. My father, you see, had taught me one thing and one thing only that I still valued. I could take almost anyone apart in a fair fight.

I decided it wasn't worth it, though. It would end up costing me more than I stood to gain, despite the satisfaction I'd get from rubbing his face in the dirt. Besides, I knew my mother wouldn't approve. Not at all.

I had met Evan Grant.

John was almost matter-of-fact about it.

"Mom found a job," he said first thing, meeting me at the door to Uncle Teddy's house after school.

I let out a whoop of joy before I could stop myself. "For sure? A real job?" I asked him, almost shaking him silly. John just nodded solemnly.

I tossed my jacket onto the nearest chair and bolted into the kitchen. "She's upstairs, Cally," my aunt said without even glancing up from the stove. "I think she's resting a bit. She was out on her feet when she came back this afternoon."

I took the stairs three at a time and burst into her bedroom without knocking. My aunt had been right. She was fast asleep, curled up in a little ball under the covers at the far end of the big double bed in the spare room.

I turned on my heels, more quietly this time, and closed the door behind me as softly as I could manage. Not that it mattered how much noise I made, it seemed, if my stampede up the stairs hadn't awakened her.

I walked back downstairs one step at a time, turning the possibilities over and over in my mind. I came up empty, in the end. I couldn't think of anything, really, my mother was qualified for.

"Oh, pish-posh," my aunt said when I voiced this

suspicion. "She's qualified for lots of things. She just doesn't know it yet."

"So what's her job?" I asked.

"Your uncle can explain it a little better than I can, I think," she said evasively.

"Well, where is it, then?" I asked impatiently.

"The State Department," she said casually.

"You're kidding?"

Aunt Franny frowned, which was always a little disconcerting. Her eyeglasses, slightly misted over from the steam in the kitchen, drooped a little down her nose and her lower lip quivered some. All in all, it was an imposing sight.

"Young man, your mother can do anything she pleases, if she has a mind to," Aunt Franny said sternly, her hands placed firmly on her rather substantial hips. "And you're to remember that, do you hear me?"

"Sure, Aunt Franny, but it's just that—"

"But nothing," she said rather loudly. "If she sets her mind to it, she can do anything. I know. I've seen her do it for years. It was always that—"

She turned away without finishing the sentence. She didn't have to, of course. We both knew precisely how she'd have finished the sentence.

My father was to blame. As always, he'd made sure my mother never reached very far. She dropped out of college just a couple of classes short of a degree so she could marry my father. She never went back to school.

Other than the fierce spiritual struggle my mother had waged for years—which really wasn't something my father could have shut down, although I'm sure he tried to—she'd never really had much of a chance to wrestle with the world.

"It's a nice place," I heard Aunt Franny saying. Her

soft, gentle voice cut through my angry reverie like a knife through butter.

"What is, Aunt Franny?" I heard myself saying.

"Where your mother will work," she said, gazing balefully at me over her drooping spectacles. "She'll like her job, I think."

Uncle Teddy was probably responsible. He ducked the question, naturally.

"Who me? Pull a few strings?" he laughed when he arrived home from work. "Would I do something like that?"

"As a matter of fact, yes," I said grumpily. My mother was still asleep and I'd now waited two hours to find out just exactly what she was going to be doing.

"Well, to be perfectly honest, I did make the introduction," he said nonchalantly. "But that's all I did. Your mother earned the job."

"So what's her job already?" I almost shouted at the top of my lungs.

"Oh, I would guess a researcher of some sort," he said breezily. "Or maybe a clerk."

"So what does that mean?"

"It means," came my mother's drowsy voice from the top of the staircase, "that I'm a GS-5, who makes only slightly more than the kid who pumps gas at the Exxon down the road."

"Marilynn," growled Uncle Teddy. "It's not quite that bad. And we've been over this and over this. To get to the top, or at least make a modest success of yourself—"

"—you have to start at the bottom," my mother finished, sighing. "I know, I know. I've heard you say it a million times."

"I'll say it a million more until you believe it," my uncle said.

"I believe it," my mother answered, rubbing the sleep from her eyes. "It just doesn't put food on the table. I have clothes to buy for the kids, you know. . . ."

"Hush!" my aunt said as she emerged from the kitchen to give her husband a hug. "No more of this talk. It's a good job. You'll like it, they'll like you, you'll get a promotion and a raise before long, and that'll be that." She paused for a moment and fixed those baleful eyes on my mother. "And you know better than that, Mrs. James. I know you're thankful beyond words that God has provided such a wonderful opportunity for you."

My mother smiled. Her eyes twinkled. "Praise the Lord," she said softly, nodding once, almost imperceptibly, in my aunt's direction.

"Will somebody please tell me what my mother will be doing for a living?" I whined like a wounded puppy.

"Filing, researching, and showing foreign dignitaries around the building," my mother said, laughing. "Not exactly what you'd call a demanding job."

Uncle Teddy shook his head violently. "Not so," he said, looking at me and not my mother. "It's a very good starting job. It will give her a chance to learn the ropes. She'll learn every corner of the place. And it will also let her know what she wants to do when she enters the Foreign Service—"

"Teddy!" my mother said sharply. "I've warned you—"

"Your mother is afraid to reach for the stars," Uncle Teddy whispered in my direction. "She's mortally afraid she might fail, so she claims she'll never take the Foreign Service exam."

"You need a formal education to take that exam," my mother said through clenched teeth. "Which I don't have. And that's the end of this discussion, I think. I'm not about to take the Foreign Service exam, much less pass it."

"You'll take it," my uncle said confidently, "in your own good time. And you'll pass it. You wait and see—"

"Enough!" my aunt said, her hands fluttering before her the way they always do when she's agitated. "Let her get settled here first, Teddy, before you start asking her to take the kids with her to some embassy in the Middle East or South America. Please?"

My mother and Uncle Teddy glanced at each other. They burst out laughing at almost the same time and agreed, through some signal only the two of them knew, that the argument had ended.

Just at that moment, for the very first time in my life, I suddenly realized that, once upon a time, Uncle Teddy had been a big brother. And my mother had been the little sister he'd always protected.

We turned John loose on Sunday, right after church.

Once upon a time—before my mom's quiet discussions about Jesus Christ had finally begun to find a place in my heart—Chris and I could usually talk our way out of it. Church, I mean. The funny thing about it was that it was dear-old-dad who usually cracked the whip, which left us to bargain with the other half.

"You're all going to Sunday School and that's that!" he'd roar at the top of his lungs. "Now get out of bed before I crack some skulls."

For awhile, we obeyed silently, without a whimper of protest. Off we'd march like cattle to count the minutes until Birmingham's version of church had ended for another Sunday.

And then dear-old-dad would hurry us into the car so we could all make it back home in time for the National Flump League. You know, grab the nearest six-pack, pop the top, and flump on the couch for the rest of the afternoon to watch the footballs fly and the beer belly grow.

Uncle Teddy, it turned out, was no soft touch. We had no choice in his household. If we didn't go to church, then raking leaves or mowing the lawn took its place. Some choice.

So it was late Sunday morning before we finally

turned John loose on the classified ads, the part where they list all the homes for rent.

Some people go through and circle all the interesting ones and then try to guess where the decent places to live are. With John, the process is far simpler. He just memorizes everything.

"Hey, John," I asked him as I studied a city map to find a street close to public tennis courts and both of the schools we'd just started in, "was there a Farnsworth Street in there anywhere?"

"Only for sale," John answered through half-closed eyes. "Two on page D17, for $157,500 and $136,000. And another one on C13—"

"OK, OK," I said quickly, before he could rattle off all the accessories the house came with. "How about Quaker Lane? Anything there?"

"Nope. Just some apartments," he answered with rare brevity.

My mother hated it when we used John for stuff like this, which was strange because he always got a big kick out of it. She said it was demeaning and made him seem like a freak or something. I thought it was a great use of his talent.

OK, OK, maybe Chris and I went a little too far the time we got him to memorize all those phone numbers in the bathrooms at a football stadium in Birmingham . . .

But this was for a noble cause. We had to find a place to live. We couldn't sponge off of Uncle Teddy forever.

"If we must do this, let's at least do it right," my mother finally sighed. "John, was there anything for rent in there under $1,000 a month?"

"Oh, sure, lots of places," John said. "On page C16, there's—"

"That's all right," she said quickly. "How about for under $750?"

He paused for a moment and screwed up his face in concentration. "There are forty-seven houses for rent less than that," he finally said. No one in the room had even the slightest bit of doubt. We'd seen John in action far too many times.

"Well, that's a relief, at least," my mother said.

"Is there anything that's, like, really low, less than $500?" I asked him. "You know, that has the word *fix* in the ad?"

John's motor clicked into action. I could almost see all those neurotransmitters passing that fine print back and forth, searching for that one word. "One with something called rent with . . . with an option to buy, whatever that means," he said at last.

"What is it, John?" my mother asked.

" 'Contractor going out of business. Forced to sell cheap. A real fix-it-yourself. Just needs some TLC,' " John said.

"What's TLC?" Jana asked.

"Tender loving care," my mother answered with a frown. "It means the place is probably half-finished and that it would take us months to fix it up."

"So let's go look at it already," Chris said impatiently. "Sounds great."

"Hardly," my mother said. "Most likely, it doesn't have any heat or any plumbing and we'll have to fit everybody into three bedrooms . . ."

"Let's just go and see it already," Chris repeated, leaping off the couch to get his coat. The rest of us weren't far behind. My mother sighed and brought up the rear after she'd made a quick call to the agent.

We all piled into the Chevy and drove away from Uncle Teddy's affluent suburb into just about one of the weirdest places I've ever seen. It was like a time warp.

Right out in the middle of all these ritzy, megabuck homes in Fairfax County is a street where all the homes are little crackerboxes, all the dogs are mangy, malnourished German shepherds, all the little kids have runny noses and mismatched shoes, all the yards look like they've been nuked, all the cars are either up on blocks or listing to one side, and all the windows are filled up with ancient eyes peering out to see who is infiltrating their crummy neighborhood this time.

You get the picture. It looked exactly like rural Alabama, transplanted about 700 miles north. I felt right at home. My mother had this sick look on her face, especially when she spotted all the empty Budweiser cans strewn across one of the yards.

But the open house we were looking for wasn't one of these. No, we had to turn off this street, plow through some underbrush, and follow an old, rutted logging trail for a ways before we came to it.

The house was sort of out in the middle of nowhere, with woods on all sides. And it was huge, absolutely monstrous, with sort of a rounded roof on top. It looked exactly like . . .

"A barn," my mother sighed, closing her eyes and shaking her head sadly. "It's an old barn somebody thought they could turn into a house."

Sure enough, off to one side was an old, rusted-out tractor plow that had sunk about halfway into the ground. The remnants of an old chicken coop were standing limply nearby and I could just make out a few sodden bales of hay on the other side of the tractor plow. What was worse, the faint aroma of cow dung still hung in the air.

"This is tough!" Chris shouted, slamming the door

open as hard as he could and charging with a full-throated battle cry towards the front of the barn/house thing. He was inside, ignoring the real estate agent, before anyone else could even get out of the car.

"What's that smell?" Jana asked, crinkling up her nose in faint disgust.

Karen gave her twin a strange look. "You've heard of cows, haven't you?"

"Is that what it is?" Jana said.

"Look down at your feet," I said with a wry smile.

"Oh, yuck," Jana said, prancing to one side before she stepped on a long-crusted cowpie.

"This is sort of gross," Susan whispered in my ear as we approached the house cautiously.

"Oh, it's not so bad," I said bravely. "Maybe it's better on the inside."

It wasn't. Not by any means. The first floor inside was just this wide expanse of wood floor slapped down to cover the dirt, wood paneling that never seemed to end, and unbelievably high ceilings criss-crossed by sturdy beams. I had the feeling that I was in an auditorium.

A long, shrieking whistle split the air above our heads. Chris had struck again. "Check it out!" he called out. I glanced up to see Chris' smiling visage peering down at us from atop a spiral staircase a long ways up and towards the back of the barn/house.

"What is it already?" Karen asked grumpily. There was no question what she thought of the place. Not that I blamed her. This place would probably be a monster to clean.

"There's a loft up here!" he shouted, his voice echoing back and forth.

"So big deal," Karen muttered.

". . . with enough room for three people," he continued, ignoring his sister's glowering stare and disparaging remarks. "It would be great for me and Cally and John—"

"Cally, John, and me," my mother corrected absentmindedly, still glancing from corner to corner far, far below him as she cradled the baby in her arms.

"Oh, come on, Mom, you wouldn't want to climb these stairs every night," Chris pleaded with just a trace of despair. He'd completely missed her point, as usual.

"You numbskull," I chided him, marveling at the way my voice carried. "She was only correcting your grammar."

"Oh," Chris said, smiling broadly as if he'd just won something.

"We are not staying here," Karen said grimly, her hands placed squarely on her hips. "No way. Not in a million years. You can't even see out the windows, they're so dirty. I'll join a convent before I move here. . . ."

"It's not so bad, Karen," Jana said in her quiet, sultry voice, the one that drove boys right out of their gourd. "Once we fixed it up and everything."

"Nothing would help this place," Karen said, casting a sour, angry glance at her twin. Jana glanced down at the floor, embarrassed that she'd crossed her sister.

"You're a real jerk sometimes," I hissed at Karen. It really bugged me sometimes the way she treated Jana, even if she was the best thing Jana had going for her sometimes.

"Yeah, and who made you the pope?" she castigated me in turn.

"There's a big window up here!" Chris shouted

again, having disappeared into the mysterious loft again.

"I still think this place is yucky," Susan whispered from my side. "But maybe I'd like it after awhile."

"We'd have to put up some walls downstairs, of course," our mother said, announcing the verdict. "And put in another bedroom probably—"

"Noooohhhh!" Karen wailed, knowing full well that my mother had already made up her mind.

"No problem," I said, trying to keep from smiling. I couldn't help it. I liked the place. It definitely had personality.

"Can I have a library?" John asked, looking directly at me.

"Sure, kid," I said, delighted that such a simple pronouncement could produce an instant, beaming smile on John's face in return.

"And the price is right," my mother said in a loud voice, taking care to fix her gaze squarely on Karen as she spoke. "We all know that has to be a consideration."

"Yes, we all know that, don't we?" I chipped in.

"Oh, shut up," Karen said, her dark, brooding eyes flashing as sharply as I've ever seen them.

"We can't afford the kind of house we had in Birmingham, babe," my mother said softly.

"Oh, I know that," Karen said sharply. "It's just that . . ."

"We'll make it nice," my mother said, taking her in with her compassionate eyes. "I promise."

Another loud shriek split the air. Chris had struck paydirt again. "Hey, great! There's even a shower up here . . ."

I was so nervous my first match that I almost double-faulted the first game away. I couldn't seem to get my serves in, so in the end I just started to throw in a bunch of second serves to keep the game going. I shouldn't have worried so much.

It was an easy match. My opponent was a seventh-grader who'd only been playing for a couple of years. I won in straight sets, 6-0, 6-0.

And after the second match—another shutout—I think I stopped worrying at all. I began to set my sights on Evan Grant.

Coach Kilmer was taking us through the formalities. He told us that if we did well, we'd get our shot at the returning varsity later in the week. But I was no longer worried about that. I wanted to play Grant. Everything else faded from view in comparison.

In fact, after my fourth match of the day, where I lost just one game, Coach Kilmer pulled me aside.

"Son, you've played tennis before?" he said, draping an arm and a clipboard over my shoulder. It was more a statement than a question.

"Yes sir, I have," I said. "Down in Birmingham. In the parks system."

"Hmm, I see," Coach Kilmer said. "And how well did you do there, down in Alabama?"

"I won the city championship last year," I answered.

"I see," he said, nodding. "That would be, what, the 14-and-under? The 16-and-under?"

"No, sir," I said quietly. "I mean the championship for the whole city. Against adults. Besides the 12-and-under, I also won the 14s twice and the 16s once too."

Coach Kilmer took his arm from my shoulder. He began to pull on his lip, a nervous habit I'd seen before. "Do you mean to say you won *the* city title there?" he said, incredulous. "Don't they have a guy down there, an amateur who's done quite well at the amateur USTA level—"

"Yeah, you mean Simon Egbert. Big guy, with a wicked first serve."

"That's right. Isn't he still down there?"

"He was seeded first the year I entered the open tournament, right after I'd won the 16s title. They gave me the last seed, just to be nice, I guess. I had to play Egbert in the round of 16."

"And you beat him?"

"I lost, in three tiebreakers," I said, smiling a little as I remembered the match. "It was pretty incredible. By the end, about a hundred people had gathered around the court to watch. All three tiebreakers were close."

Coach Kilmer just stared at me as if I were crazy. "And the next year?"

"I beat him in straight sets," I said simply. "After I played him that first time, I worked like a dog on my return of serve. I couldn't stand being out of games, unable to get the ball back into play."

"And how'd you practice against a serve like that?"

I gave him a cockeyed grin. "It was easy, actually. I worked in the parks system that summer, so every night I just borrowed our one and only ball machine, set it up on a platform on the other side of the net, cranked it up full power and shot balls down into the service court at weird angles. After that, real serves seemed almost easy to go get."

"You seem to take your tennis pretty seriously... Carl," he said after glancing down at his clipboard to remember my name.

"Yes, sir, I do. And my name's Cally," I said.

"OK, Cally," he said. "I'll try to remember. And I'll see you out here tomorrow?"

"You bet. I'll be here."

*   *   *   *   *

The second day of tryouts was even easier, if you can believe it. I only played two matches and I didn't lose a single game in four straight sets. I was beginning to believe Uncle Teddy, that I could make the team.

But, like I said, I didn't just want to make the team. I wanted Evan Grant, or at least a shot at him. The idea was at the back of my mind as I hit every shot. I sometimes caught myself thinking of ways to counter Grant's consistency right in the middle of a point.

When Coach Kilmer read the list of kids who'd get their chance to play the returning varsity for places on the team, I acknowledged my name with a small smile.

"Be here at 4 sharp tomorrow," the coach said to the six of us who'd run the gauntlet so far. "I'll give you your assignments then."

*   *   *   *   *

I rose through the ranks. Quickly. In fact, I didn't lose a set on my rapid ascent to the top of the team's "ladder." By the time I'd come within reach of Evan Grant, the rest of the players had simply stopped talking to me. I might as well have been a leper.

I could understand their reaction, I guess. They'd

gone to the state championships the year before with the squad they now had. They didn't need anyone else to make it back. Anything that changed the balance, in their minds, could only upset chemistry.

I didn't say anything, of course. That probably made matters worse, of course. These guys had no idea who I was, working my way to the top towards their fearless leader with such impunity.

It was a Friday—the third week into the school year—when I finally made it to Bill Hunter, a short, squat kid who played number two and who seemed to delight in giving Coach Kilmer grief.

It was a windy day, exactly the wrong kind of a day for someone who likes long rallies. It was just too hard to keep the ball in consistently. I felt sorry for Hunter. He relied too much on consistency, like Evan Grant. He tended to scramble around the court, just trying to keep the ball in and hoping that his opponent didn't make a mistake.

For my part, I decided to play the margins. I wouldn't cut it close down the line or when I hit it deep. I wouldn't need that. A decent first serve and steady pressure on his backhand should do the trick.

As we warmed up, I almost smiled as Hunter tried to rocket the ball back at me with each return. I *knew* he wouldn't hit that way during the match. Some players leave their best shots in practice and Hunter was one of those players. *Me*, I tend to take it easy as I warm up. I don't turn it loose until the game actually begins.

I noticed, out of the corner of my eye, that the rest of the squad was paying an extraordinary amount of attention to our match. A few even stared. Well, fine, no problem.

It was over quickly. Hunter picked up maybe two

dozen points in two sets. He was hopelessly out-matched. By the middle of the second set I think he'd resigned himself to that fact, because he started try-ing to hit the ball back as hard as he could. Balls flew out right and left.

To his credit, Hunter took it in stride. When it was all over — 6-0, 6-0 — he walked to the net slowly, a lop-sided grin spreading across his face. "You killed me," he said, reaching for my outstretched hand.

"Hey, I'm sorry . . ."

"Forget that," Hunter said, his grin getting even wider. "Don't be sorry just 'cause you blew me away. We can use you on the team. No question. We're gonna win state with you around."

"But everyone's avoiding me," I said, giving him a strange look.

"Sure, they're avoiding you. They were scared stiff about you. But, man, you wiped us all out and there ain't nothin' any of us can do about it. Ain't nothin' to be afraid of, either."

"I was just trying to make the team," I said, shrugging.

Hunter laughed. "Yeah, I guess you made it. So wel-come aboard." He held his hand out. I shook it, again.

9

It was funny the way my mother started to study for the Foreign Service exam. She did it in secret, when she thought no one would know.

And when is that, with seven kids screaming for your constant attention? Where do you find five minutes to yourself, much less an hour?

You find it at midnight, that's when. You give up a couple of hours of sleep—and shorten your life a little—to put the studying time in.

Of course, if my mother thought she was pulling something over on us she had another thing coming. Oh, I suppose she *thought* she could get away with it. But all mothers are like that.

Susan came tiptoeing into my room the first night my mother tried her new plan out.

"Cally," this small voice said in the darkness of my room.

"Go away," Chris said gruffly from the bunk below me.

"Wasn't talkin' to you," Susan said sweetly.

"Don't care," Chris mumbled.

I cut the argument short, now that I was awake. "What's up, Sue?" I asked, leaning down over the side of the top bunk.

Susan walked over and tried to pull herself up. I grabbed her by the arms and lifted her the rest of the way. "Mommy's up," she whispered.

"What do you mean she's up?"

"I heard her 'larm clock go off."

I glanced over at the clock on my dresser. It was almost one in the morning. "You're sure?"

"Yep. I heard it, and then I checked. She's down in the kitchen."

"What's she doin'?"

"She's got all these books spread out on the table. If you don't believe it, follow me, I'll show you."

It took me a second or two—or three—before it came to me why she was down there. "Let's go see," I said, smiling.

"But we can't let her see us," Susan said as she hoisted herself down over the side and dropped softly to the floor. "Promise?"

"OK," I said as I lowered myself down. "We'll be secret agents."

"You're both nuts," Chris said as he slammed a pillow over his head.

We climbed down the stairs from the loft, the house's third level, and then tiptoed down the hallway as quietly as we could, missing all the creaking boards with a deftness that came from practice.

We both saw the light around the corner as we descended the second flight of stairs. I glanced down at Susan. A look of deadly earnest was plastered on her face. She was genuinely concerned about this.

As we came to the final corner before the kitchen, Susan suddenly lowered herself to the ground and slid across the floor on her stomach. As she peered around the corner that way, I slowly leaned my head out and looked into the dimly lit kitchen.

My mother did, indeed, have some books spread out in front of her on the kitchen table. I couldn't tell what they were, but I didn't have to. I knew what they were.

Susan and I both pulled back. "See?" she said to me soundlessly.

I just nodded and motioned her back up the stairs. "You were right," I said at the top.

"Cally, what's she doin'?" Susan asked with a small note of urgency in her voice.

I thought about the small dream my mother now nurtured deep, deep down in her soul right now, a dream that seemed to make almost no sense in her present circumstances. "She's studying for somethin' really important," I told my sister.

"For what?"

"Somethin' to do with her work. She has to take a test."

"What kind of a test?"

I decided to head Susan off at the pass. Her questions would never end, not right now. And I didn't want to panic her with the thought of moving to the Middle East or Africa . . .

"It's a test so she can get a promotion at work. Now, Sue, you have to promise me?" Susan nodded before I'd even told her what she had to promise. "You can't tell anyone about this. It's our secret, OK?"

"OK, I promise," she vowed solemnly.

"That's a good girl," I said, thankful that I'd managed to derail her stream of questions. "Now, go back to sleep. And when you hear her alarm clock from now on, just roll over and go back to sleep. Got it?"

She nodded again. ". . . Cally?" she said, finally.

"What?"

"If Mommy passes this test, is she gonna move us all again to some other part of the world? And will Daddy be there?"

I sighed to myself very silently. This was not my department. Not at all. I think it belongs to someone else, like a parent or something. "No, Susan, I don't think Mom's gonna move us. We're here to stay for awhile."

I couldn't tell if it was hope or despair that crossed her face for an instant. But it was soon gone, replaced by a look of acceptance. And as she turned to go back to her bedroom, I could see the wheels spinning madly inside her small head.

10

"Mom, you look awful," Karen said at breakfast the next morning.

"Karen!" my aunt said sharply, "that's not nice."

"But it's true," Karen said with a sour, sidelong glance at Aunt Franny. "And you're not my mother, so quit tryin' to lecture me."

My mother blanched. Something was really eating away at Karen. I figured I knew what it was. For a reason I couldn't fathom, I had this feeling she really missed our worthless father. I'll bet Karen even thought Mom was responsible. She's goofy about things like that.

Aunt Franny, who was there to look after the baby for when Mom was at work, moved in quickly. "We wouldn't dream of lecturing you, Karen. You're much too smart for us," she said easily.

"Franny, don't baby her like that," my mother said with a sigh. She turned her gaze back to Karen. "And as for you, young lady, if I *ever* hear you speak to your aunt like that again . . ."

"You'll what? Spank me?" Karen said, her face beginning to contort with rage. "Go ahead. I don't care."

My mother was silent. We all were. This just wasn't like Karen. I understood her anger, more than a little. But this made no sense.

"I think we'll take this up later," my mother said

softly, letting her eyes linger a little on Karen before glancing at the rest of us around the breakfast table. "Now, finish up. The school bus'll be here soon."

Karen sulked through the rest of breakfast. Thankfully, the conversation quickly turned in other directions.

John was having trouble with English. It was bizarre. He'd remember every page from the stories he read, word for word. But when he had to tell the teacher what the stories actually *meant*, well, he was lost.

Chris had been seen holding a girl's hand. Jana had spotted the two of them on the way home from school and I guess she decided it was something the entire family needed to know about. Chris blushed, if you can believe that. Then he flicked some of his oatmeal at her.

Two guys had already asked Jana out. She wasn't allowed to date yet, but that didn't seem to stop anyone from asking. I usually relied on Karen to tell me what Jana was doing, but Karen wasn't talking these days. So I was having a tough time keeping track of Jana.

So what was making Karen crazy inside? I mean, I knew she was the only one of us who really got along with our father, but even she knew what he was like, what he'd done to the family. No way could she, deep down, blame our mother for what happened.

I decided that, maybe, it was time I found out what was going on. "Hey, Karen," I said as we made our way to the corner, where the school bus always picked us up. "Gotta second?"

Karen shrugged and moved away from the other kids waiting for the bus. "I'm not goin' anywhere."

I took that as an invitation. "What's the deal? Why'd

you give Mom such a hard time back there?"

"You aren't my father," she snapped, her eyes boring into mine. "So don't even try to give me a lecture or anything."

I decided to gamble. "No, but, um, have you heard from him lately?"

I could see that the question really surprised her. She tried to hide it, but I could see. Karen and I really couldn't keep secrets between us. "Dad? Heard from Dad?" she managed to ask.

"Yeah, him," I persisted. "Have you heard from him lately?"

Karen took a quick, almost desperate, glance down the street to see if the school bus might rescue her. No such luck. She'd have to answer my question.

"What if I have?" she said evasively.

"Have you told Mom?" I asked. "Does she know that you've called him?"

"I never called him," Karen said quickly.

"Then how . . ."

Karen has a bad temper when she gets angry. She was starting to get angry. "He called me at school. Got me out of class," she said curtly.

"He called you at *school?*" I asked, incredulous. "How'd he find you?"

"Beats me. I didn't ask. He knew we were stayin' at Uncle Teddy's, so he probably called around to all the schools here."

"So what did he want to talk about?"

"Oh, nothin' much. What we were doin,' how Mom was. Stuff like that."

"And you just talked to him?"

Karen's eyes flashed. "And what was I *supposed* to do, just hang up on him? He is our *father,* or have you forgotten?"

Off in the distance, I could hear the gears of the ancient Thompson Elementary school bus grinding away. Any minute now, it would turn the corner and make its way down the road we lived on. I pressed on quickly.

"I haven't forgotten," I said, matching Karen's tone. "But he ran out on us, not the other way around."

Karen hesitated. "You know, he . . . he's left the girl he was livin' with," she finally blurted out.

Sudden, raw anger coursed through me. *As if that made a difference,* I thought miserably. "So what?" I answered. "It doesn't make it right. I don't care if he goes off and lives like a monk. It won't change things."

Karen narrowed her eyes mischievously. "But what about forgiving others, like Mom says?" she prodded. "Hasn't she been talkin' to you about all that born-again Christian stuff, pointing things out in the Bible?"

"I don't think . . ."

"Aren't Christians supposed to forgive others?" she repeated.

The school bus was slowly chugging up the hill. "Well, I guess. But I'm not really a Christian yet. I mean, everything Mom's talking about is pretty inter-esting. I like it. But I don't know if I believe in it all."

"Oh, phooey," she said crisply. "Sure you do. I know you do. Which means that you're supposed to forgive crummy people. Like Dad."

Karen was wrong. I don't think I would ever forgive our father. Not ever. Not even if he crawled back on his hands and knees and vowed never to do anything rotten again for the rest of his life. "Maybe you can forgive him," I said with some finality. "I can't."

Karen's school bus creaked to a stop in front of us.

The other kids from the neighborhood began to pile onto the bus. Oblivious to this, Karen stepped to the rear of the line and began to edge her way towards the bus door.

"You know," she said slowly, quietly, so no one else would hear. "There's something else . . ."

"What?"

"Dad said he's comin' back to see us."

"Coming back? Here?"

"He didn't say when, or where," Karen said conspiratorially. "He just said he was comin' back to see us. He didn't say any more than that."

A giant, gaping hole began to open up in the bottom of my stomach. "He better not look me up," I said through clenched teeth. "He better not."

"But you know he will," Karen said as she began to vanish into the bus. "You know he will."

I guess I did know that. But now I would be ready for him.

11

I couldn't sleep again, of course, the night before my big match. Pictures of Evan Grant returning my shots endlessly, effortlessly, rolled through my mind like a movie reel with an endless loop.

It was torture, really, trying to develop any strategy against him. He was like a backboard. I just had to assume he'd return anything and everything.

Now, I knew there had to be a way to beat him. He had to have some flaws in his game. No one's perfect. At least, no one that I know.

The trouble was, I wasn't sure I had the patience to find the flaws. I knew I had the stamina and the determination. Patience, though, isn't something I was blessed with.

I like the power point, where I can take a serve and drill it down the line for a winner; or where I serve, rush the net, and pounce on the return for an easy winner.

I wouldn't be able to do that with Evan Grant. He was too crafty, too relentless, too sure-footed, too confident, too quick, too . . .

"Would you *stop* that," Chris hissed loudly in the still night.

"What?"

"All that thinkin', that's what," he said. "I can hear it down here."

"I'm not . . ."

"Oh, *please*. You've turned over a thousand zillion times, and the bed creaks every time you do."

"I can't help that. Oil it or something."

"You oil it. It's your brain that's makin' all the racket."

"Ha, ha. Real funny."

"What's funny?"

"All the racket . . ."

Chris giggled. "Oh, hey. That was an accident."

"Yeah, well, if you don't let me go to sleep, you'll be an accident," I growled, rolling over for the thousand zillion and first time.

"I don't know what you're all worried about," Chris kidded. "He's gonna murder you, anyway."

"No, he won't," I said fiercely.

"Then quit worryin' and go back to sleep."

I didn't, of course. By the time the sun finally grabbed the bottom of our window and pulled itself into view, I'd accumulated a grand total of maybe two hours of sleep. Oh well.

My body ached, I was so tired. I managed only a few bites of Cream of Wheat before my school bus came. I almost missed it. I had to run around the house like a crazy man gathering up my books and stuff, and then cut through four backyards to catch the bus before it turned the corner.

Every class that day was pure, raw agony. I squirmed, fidgeted, and fought off sleep through every lecture. Waiting for the end of the day to come and tennis practice to begin was murder.

Finally, after what seemed like another thousand zillion years, gym class arrived. I only had one more period—biology—after gym, so I'd made it. I could survive biology. Then it would be time for Evan Grant.

Time to test myself, to see if I was really as good as I thought I was.

It was funny, but I sort of avoided Evan Grant and his pals in the locker room as we got dressed for class. I guess I didn't want to look him in the eye until we were on the court. I had the funny feeling that he was avoiding me too, for exactly the same reason.

His entourage was in full force, though. All his pals kept their eyes glued on me. They followed every move I made, as if there was something special about putting your gym clothes on.

Our gym teacher, Coach Petit, had made Evan and me the captains of the two gym teams. Everybody on my team had picked up the unspoken rivalry with Evan Grant. Every time we faced off against his team—no matter what the sport was—it was a war. Both teams scrapped and clawed and fought for victory.

If it was volleyball, we'd dive for balls until our knees were raw. If it was softball, we'd slide headfirst and risk the red welts on our legs. If it was basketball, the elbows flew in all directions.

It was as if our personal rivalry—a rivalry that had more to do with sidelong glances, scowls, and gritted teeth than actual hand-to-hand combat—had become part of something larger.

In fact, I'm sure that's just what Coach Petit had in mind when he put Evan Grant at the head of one team and me at the other. He was a good coach, and he could spot an old-fashioned feud when he saw one.

As we made our way out of the locker room to the gym floor, one of Evan Grant's pals—Johnny Clark—sidled up beside me. Barely, out of the corner of one eye, I'd seen Evan Grant say something to him before he moved off quickly in my direction to catch up to me.

I bristled as Clark moved with me. He was a real

character. I had no idea why Evan Grant palled around with him. I guess it didn't matter to Grant, as long as his "friends" were loyal to him.

Johnny Clark always smoked a cigarette in the restroom right around the corner from the gym during classes. No one ever used that restroom anymore. It smelled like a sewer because it was practically reserved for the kids who thought smoking was cool.

About every week or so, somebody pulled one of the fire alarms. Invariably, you'd see Clark racing around the corner after it happened, though he was never caught at it.

Still, Clark was in and out of the principal's office all the time. Like the time he was caught skulking around in the girl's locker room before school began. I can only guess what Clark was doing in there.

It was funny. Just the night before, my mom and I had read from the Bible about loving your enemies, about "doing good" to those who hate you.

Oh, yeah. I was starting to sit down with Mom at night—after John, Susan, and Timmy were in bed—just to talk about things. Just talk, though. I still wasn't committing to anything.

Anyway, in this part of the Bible, Jesus also talks about blessing those who curse you and praying for those who abuse you. Then comes the worst part. If someone hits you with a right hook on one side of the face, you're supposed to turn your face so he can whack you on the other side.

No way. I'll never become a Christian, not if I have to do that, I thought. *Never mind that God is supposed to help you with things like that, with the really hard parts. I still can't just let somebody beat on me, no matter how much God helps me.*

Somehow, I knew instinctively that Johnny Clark

qualified as an enemy. It wasn't anything he *said*. I just knew. I have this funny sort of gift I was born with. I can always seem to figure out where people are coming from when I meet them. And Johnny Clark was up to no good.

"Hey, Deep South," Clark hissed beside me. "Wanna hear somethin'?"

"Not really," I answered casually.

"Hey, no problem," he shrugged. "Maybe I'll just tell you anyway."

"Maybe I don't care."

"Oh, you'll *care*," Clark said with an evil smirk. "I guarantee that."

"You think so?"

"I know so. I can tell 'bout things like this."

I kept moving. I had this sudden urge to stop, right there on the ramp up to the gym floor, and square off against him. Something about the guy made me uneasy. Just thinking about it made me move a little quicker.

"Hey, don't run off just yet, Deep South," he said quickly. "I got somethin' to tell ya."

"Look," I said, slowing a little, just enough to let him catch up to me again. "I already told you . . ."

"Jana," Clark said, cutting me off. "That's your sweet sister's name, isn't it? Jana? Over at Thompson Elementary?"

My blood froze. My mind moved into hyperspace. Time seemed to stand still for a fraction of a moment. "Yeah. So?" It was all I could do to keep myself from shaking in fury.

"Oh, nothin', really," he answered. "It's just that I seen her when I was over there. She was sweet to me. Real sweet. She's a cute kid."

I almost reached out and grabbed him, but he'd already moved away by the time I'd come to grips with what he'd said. What did he mean he'd *seen* her? What did that mean, exactly? Jana had been *sweet* to him?

The shrill burst of a whistle broke my thought. Coach Petit was standing in the middle of the floor, the whistle jutting out of his mouth. "Let's go, folks!" he barked. "You're late!"

The rest of the kids hustled out of the locker room and assembled on the floor in less than a minute. I took my place out in front, beside Evan Grant and facing everyone else.

"Start it, James!" Coach Petit yelled in my direction.

I nodded, and yelled at my sluggish peers, "Fifty jumping jacks! Ready? Begin!" The rhythmic *thump, slap, thump, slap* of the exercise almost distracted me. Almost, but not quite.

My eyes tried to find Clark's, but he wasn't having any of that. He was joking with somebody and half-heartedly doing the exercise. I saw him hack once. Clark was always out of breath from all the smoking he did.

The jumping jacks ended and Evan Grant picked up the next exercise. "Twenty push-ups!" he bellowed in his deepest voice. "Ready? Hit it!" In unison, we all plunked to the ground and did our push-ups to Grant's "one . . . two . . . one . . . two" count.

"Roll over!" I yelled at the conclusion of the push-ups. "Thirty sit-ups! Ready, begin!"

At the apex of every sit-up, I tried to catch Clark's eye. He wouldn't bite. He wasn't even doing his sit-ups. He'd only go part way down and then come back up. No wonder he was in such lousy shape, I thought fleetingly.

But when the exercises were over and it was time

for our laps around the gym, I saw my chance. Usually, I tore around the gym at the front of the pack. Today, though, I'd have to pull up the rear in order to hang back with Clark and the other wheezers in the class.

My teeth hurt, I was clenching them so hard when I slowed my stride to match Clark's leisurely pace. I worked my way in beside him. Two other kids moved off to the side to let me in.

"What do you mean, you *saw* her?" I said, my voice low, dangerous.

Clark almost grinned. "Like I told ya, Deep South," he wheezed. "When I was over at Thompson. I go there all the time."

I could feel the prickles on the back of my neck. "What's at Thompson?" I asked, already knowing the answer.

"Ya ain't that stupid, Deep South," he answered under his breath. "They got plenty of real sweet girls. Just like your Jana."

"No way," I said. "They wouldn't let you come around over there."

"Sure they do," he smirked. "Who's gonna stop me? I go over there all the time, just to pick out the pretty ones."

"They wouldn't let you on the school grounds," I persisted.

"Don't need to go on the grounds," Clark answered. "They all come to *me*. For smokes. Out in the woods behind the cafeteria during lunch."

"You're crazy," I said.

Clark slowed even more. We dropped all the way to the rear of the pack, just the two of us. The run was almost over; I could see Evan Grant streaking towards the finish on the other side of the gym.

"That's where I saw her," he said quietly, turning his face to look at me as he said it. "Your sister, Jana. She was out back with me. Like I said, she was real sweet to me. I mean, real nice and—"

He never finished the sentence. I put a right hook into his chin just as the last of his words were trailing out. He dropped almost instantly, blood from his mouth spurting all over the floor.

Clark rolled over as soon as he'd hit the floor. He scrambled towards me and grabbed my legs. Before I could react, we were both on the floor. Clark fought like a junkyard dog, gouging and kicking and butting his head. I put in a few more licks before Coach Petit raced over.

"Enough, you two!" the coach yelled.

I began to relax, glad the fight was over. Clark, though, just kept plowing ahead. He didn't let up at all. Before I could stop him, he gave me a sharp elbow to my ribs.

"Hey," I said, grimacing. The pain shot up one side and through my shoulder blade. Clark just kept coming. He was like a freight train out of control. Kids started to gather around us.

"I said hold it!" Coach Petit bellowed. I was all for that, but Clark wouldn't let up. After a punch below the belt, I rejoined the fight. I wasn't about to let him get away with murder. I sent an uppercut into his jaw. Clark grunted as the impact rattled a few teeth.

Kids started to grab us, trying to pull us apart. Clark held onto me for dear life, kicking at my shins furiously.

"Stop it right now, or I'm sending the two of you to the principal's office!" Coach Petit tried yet again. Clark just redoubled his efforts.

It was several long minutes later when they finally

pried us apart. Clark was bloody all over. His face was smeared with the stuff. Mostly, I just had blood from his mouth all over my shirt. You could tell where he bit me because the blood stains were a deep red.

Angry beyond words, Coach Petit ordered several kids to bring the two of us with him. He began to troop off to the principal's office.

I shrugged off my handlers. "I can do it myself," I said sourly. I caught a smiling Evan Grant in the background as I was leaving the gym.

Once we were in the outer office, Coach Petit quickly ushered us past the secretary right into where the principal was sitting. Kamber looked up, mildly surprised at the sight, as we walked in.

"So what have we here?" he asked.

"A fight," Coach Petit said simply. "A nasty one too. It completely disrupted my class."

"I see," Kamber said. "So. What do you have to say for yourselves?"

Clark stuck his jaw out. Blood was already starting to cake to it. "He hit me first. For no reason at all," he said quickly.

Kamber glanced at me. "Is that true? Did you hit him first?"

I almost thought about arguing. But I knew it was hopeless. It wouldn't do anyone any good to talk about defending your sister's honor. No one ever cares about stuff like that.

"Yes, sir, I did," I answered.

"And why did you do that?" Kamber asked.

I looked over at Clark, who was smirking. "Because I didn't like something he said," I replied.

"That's all? Because you didn't like something he said?"

"Yes, sir. That's all."

It was obvious to Kamber that he wasn't going to get an explanation of what happened. He'd had Clark in here before, and he never confessed. So, if I wasn't talking, then he knew he'd gotten all there was to get.

"All right," Kamber said. "I don't really have a choice. You both know fighting in school is against the rules. I'm going to have to suspend both of you for three days, beginning today. I'll notify your teachers."

"But I have a match . . ." I began to protest.

Kamber raised his hand. "Son, you had your chance. You admitted you started the fight. I don't have a choice. You're both suspended."

I looked over at Clark. He was grinning from ear to ear like a village idiot. A gnawing suspicion that I'd been taken to the cleaners began to work its way into the back of my mind.

You see, not only would this keep me from meeting Evan Grant on the court, I was pretty sure the suspension would force me off the tennis team. I was done, finished, for the year.

In one inglorious moment, my hopes had faded to nothing. My mother and Uncle Teddy would just be sick. Chris would be crushed.

And me? Well, I wasn't real sure what I would do next.

12

"Don't despair. There's always next year," Uncle Teddy said as we drove home from school. I'd called him—not Mom—because I wasn't ready to tell the family about the fight just yet.

Always hopeful, always optimistic, always ready to find the silver lining in even the darkest cloud, that's Uncle Teddy.

"But I was right *there*," I said emphatically. "I was so close."

There was a long pause as Uncle Teddy stared out at the road deep in thought. "Well, hmmm, let me see. Maybe there is something ..."

"What?" I asked anxiously. "Do you know somebody? Can you get me back into school?"

"Cally, Cally," my uncle said softly. "No. I can't get your suspension lifted. Even if I could, I don't think I would."

"But ..."

"You were wrong. Dead wrong, Cally," he said. "Your punishment may be a little harsh, but you were still wrong. We all have to pay for our mistakes. You're just paying a stiffer fine than most because it affects something you care about so deeply."

I was confused. "But you said there was something ...?"

"Yes, I did, but it has nothing to do with school," he

said mysteriously. "I don't think we should talk about it right now, though. I don't want to get your hopes up. Let me work on it for a little bit and I'll get back to you. OK?"

"Sure," I said glumly. What choice did I have?

I waited until all the kids were home before I let any of them know what had happened. I tried the news out on Karen first, mostly because she's usually the most level-headed.

"Yeah, I've seen him," she said after I'd finished my story. "He's always out back, behind the cafeteria, smoking away like a fiend. He's a real dope. Nobody likes him or anything."

"And Jana? What about her?"

Karen scowled. "I'm almost positive Jana's never been back there. I think I'd know about it if she had been."

"You're sure?"

"Pretty sure," Karen said with a shrug. "Jana sometimes hangs out with some weird kids. But that guy's a real creep. There's no way. She'd never hang out with somebody like him, not in a million years."

So. I really had been taken to the cleaners. Somebody had set me up. They knew what would get to me. And like a master puppeteer who knows which string to pull at which moment in the drama, Evan Grant had remained far above the action, controlling our actions.

It made me so mad I couldn't see straight. In fact, by the time I walked into Karen and Jana's room, I'd almost forgotten about Johnny Clark. He wasn't the enemy. I knew the enemy now.

"Jana, do you know a kid named Johnny Clark?" I asked, plopping myself down on the corner of her bed. Jana looked up from her homework.

It was amazing, actually. Of all the kids in the family, Jana was the most diligent about getting to her homework first thing after school. I think she did it because it gave her time to talk on the phone all night.

"Does he go to Thompson?"

I shook my head. "He goes to Roosevelt, with me, but he sometimes hangs out behind Thompson during lunch."

That struck a chord. "Oh, yeah, sure. I've seen him out there before. Some of the kids go out there to smoke."

"Have, um, have *you* ever been back there?" I asked cautiously.

Jana laughed. It took me by surprise. "Come on. You're kidding, right?"

"So you've never actually met this kid, Johnny Clark?"

"Nah. He just likes to think he's cool, 'cause he goes to Roosevelt now. But nobody I know likes him or anything." Jana turned back to her books. I'd heard enough.

"Thanks, Jana," I said, moving towards the door.

"Sorry about tennis," she said over her shoulder, her nose still buried in her books. Karen had already told her about the fight.

"Yeah, well that's life, I guess," I grimaced.

Chris, as I'd expected, was hopping mad. And I mean literally hopping mad. I think he bruised one of his feet stomping around our room after I broke the news to him.

"Why'd you do *that!*" he yelled when I told him how I'd punched Clark in the jaw.

"What do you mean, why? You'd have done the same thing," I said.

"But now you can't play tennis," Chris said shaking

his head sadly. "Man, that's one of your all-time *dumb* moves."

"I know, and there have been plenty of them."

John and Susan took it gracefully. They didn't care. No, that's not exactly right. Susan was thrilled, because it meant I could spend more time at home with her after school for the next three days before I went to the racquet club. John put the information in his computer brain and concluded that what I'd done was, well, wrong.

Having purged my soul by confessing to my brothers and sisters, I couldn't take any more. I grabbed my basketball and walked around the corner to a nearby park and shot baskets aimlessly until it got too dark to see where the ball was going.

I completely missed dinner, of course. I was seriously thinking of skipping sleep that night as well. Maybe I could just sort of wander around for the rest of the night.

In fact, maybe I could just grab a few bags of chips and Ding-Dongs from the 7-Eleven and hang out somewhere, anywhere, for the next three days. It seemed like a marvelous idea. Totally impractical, but marvelous.

You see, I just *knew* she'd be waiting for me. My mother, I mean. She'd be doing the dishes in the kitchen, or sewing a button on one of Jana's shirts, or reading a book to Susan, or nursing Timmy, or refereeing a fight between Karen and Chris.

But she'd still be there, waiting. And I didn't quite know what I would tell her. Really and truly, I was beginning to hear what she'd been telling me about Jesus. It was beginning to make sense. And now . . .

But how can I get it right every time? How can you really expect that? You can't. It's impossible. I just

knew I'd be making mistakes — including a few whop-
pers like today's — for the rest of my life.

I knew there was no way that *I* could keep myself
on the straight and narrow. *Now, Cally,* I could hear
my mother say to me, *that's the marvelous thing about
what Jesus said, what He promised. God knows you
will fail. We all fail.*

She would tell me, again, that all have sinned and
fall short of the glory of God, and that we can only be
"redeemed" by grace through Jesus.

If we believe that, and ask Jesus to help us, to bring
us near to God, then all of those sins will be forgiven
and we can begin to learn how to walk *with* God. We
don't stop making mistakes, my mother would say.
We just begin to learn how to stop making so *many* of
them.

I guess that makes sense. It didn't put me back on
the tennis team, though. And it didn't make it any
easier to face my mother right now.

"Oh, well," I said out loud to no one in particular in
the middle of the darkening park. "Might as well get it
over with." *And God,* I added silently, *I know You're
listening to me. I think I'm gonna need some help on
this one. Lots of it.*

The "barn," as Chris affectionately called our house,
looked unusually cheery and bright from the outside
as I approached it. In fact, it looked downright invit-
ing. Which made the burden I was carrying even
heavier, of course.

There was no one to greet me at the door. There
was no one in the living room just off the foyer, or in
the den either. But I could hear muffled shouts and
bursts of laughter coming through the door that led
down to the rec room in our partially finished
basement.

"AAAgggghhh!" I heard Chris shout as I walked slowly down the stairs.

"Serves you right, for smashing Susan," I heard Karen say.

"I did *not* smash Susan," Chris protested.

"Here comes the serve!" I heard my mother say, outshouting both Chris and Karen.

I turned the corner and just stopped dead in my tracks, too amazed for words. Every single member of our family—except for Timmy, who was fast asleep upstairs, no doubt—was gathered around the beatup Ping-Pong table Uncle Teddy had given us a few weeks ago.

I saw my mother serve and then move to her right. Jana returned the serve, and then started to move to her right as John returned her shot and moved to *his* right. By this time, Karen had moved in behind Jana to return John's shot. She hit the ball to Chris, who returned it to Susan.

Then it just started going faster and faster, with each member of my family beginning to run pell mell around the Ping-Pong table trying to keep up until Chris tried to slam the ball and missed the end of the table. Again, apparently.

"Oh, phooey!" Chris yelled, jumping high and almost bonking his head on the low ceiling in the room.

It was all so very strange. I'd never seen our family do anything quite like this before. I mean, not the whole, entire family all at once. It was like a party, without me.

"Come on over," my mother yelled at me as she picked the ball up off the floor and began to serve.

"Yeah, grab a paddle and get in line in front of me," Karen said. "We need somebody who can hit it back hard at Chris. He keeps slamming Susan."

"I do *not* keep slamming Susan," Chris tried to protest again. "You just keep setting me up and I can't help myself."

No way was I going to be left out of this. "That'll change now, Ace," I said with a cockeyed grin. Chris just scowled as I grabbed a paddle and moved in front of Karen.

It was almost enough to make me forget what I'd managed to do to myself earlier in the day. Almost. And, you know, I'll bet that's exactly what my mother had in mind.

Needless to say, I took the very first opportunity to put Chris away and make him pay for what he'd done to Susan. On my first trip around the table, I took John's high, looping shot and smashed it viciously to my left. Chris dove for it, but never came close.

"This isn't fair!" Chris hollered as he landed on the ground with a thud and careened into the baseboard. He began to vigorously massage his right elbow as he picked himself off the ground.

"It is too fair," Karen shot back. "You've been picking on Susan all night."

"Have not," Chris said. "I can't help it if she's next in line . . . "

"Well, now I can't help it if you're in line in front of *me,*" I said, smiling broadly, my cares and woes fading as rapidly as the conversation's pace. "Your serve."

Chris grimaced, swiped the ball from the floor and served it viciously. It skidded off the end of the table.

"Hey!" Susan said as she lunged for the serve. She barely got her paddle on the ball, but it was enough to send it back to the other side in a lazy arc. We all began to move around the table again.

Chris was ready for me the next time around. He

anticipated my smash to the left and hastily moved that way before I hit. Which led me to hit a backhand to my *right*. He never touched the ball.

"You're all ganging up on me," Chris said mournfully as the ball ricocheted around in the corner.

"You're just too slow," Jana teased.

"Yeah, can't you move any faster?" John chimed in. Chris was really in deep trouble if John—who was dead serious—was piling on too.

Chris just glowered at both of them. "You're crazy. Cally's gonna kill me every time if you guys keep settin' him up like that."

"You deserve it," Susan said, her chin jutting out.

"I do not," Chris said.

"All right, all right," said our mother, the referee. "There's no need to pick on Chris."

The game began again. This time, though, Chris bounced a nice, easy serve in Susan's direction.

"There!" Chris said with a huff.

"That's better," Susan said as she sort of shoveled the ball back to the other side.

"That's nice," my mother pronounced, and then proceeded to miss most of the ball. It caught the top of her paddle, flew straight up in the air, and slammed into the low ceiling with a loud "pop."

Somewhere in the back of my mind, even as I was rolling with laughter along with all the other kids, I found myself wondering if maybe she hadn't purposefully missed the ball to make peace in the family. That would be just like her. . . .

* * * * * *

My mother waited up with me. I knew she would, of course. I was sure Uncle Teddy, or someone else perhaps, had filled her in on what had happened at school. But she'd want to hear it from me. No matter how painful, she always demanded a full confession.

"Why don't we go for a walk?" she said after she'd read the next chapter of *The Lion, the Witch and the Wardrobe* to Susan and then tucked her in.

"But what about Timmy?" I asked. "You won't be able to hear him if he cries."

"Karen will listen for him," she said quickly. She opened the closet door and pulled both of our coats off their hangers. She tossed mine in my face. "Let's go, kid."

"OK," I said. I put my coat on in a hurry and began to move towards the front door.

"No, let's go out back, through the woods," my mother said. "I don't feel like walking through the streets."

The cool evening had a slight chill to it now. It was about that time of night when the temperature starts to drop, no matter how warm the day has been.

My mother linked one of her arms through mine. That's something she hardly ever does. Usually, I'd get real embarrassed over something like that. Tonight, it just seemed like the right thing to do.

We walked like that, in silence, for a long time, wandering under branches and catching occasional glimpses of the bright stars and the clear moon.

We followed a path in a clearing that led to a small, wooden bridge. My mother stopped and leaned against one of the railings. I moved over to the other side and leaned against a post.

"So. You got kicked out of school," she said quietly.

"For fighting."

"For fighting," she said, nodding.

"I didn't mean to, Mom. It just sort of happened."

"I know, Cally. I know you'd never do something like that on purpose," said my mother, whose eyes were unnaturally bright and piercing right now. I looked away. I couldn't face those eyes, not right now.

"I feel pretty stupid right now," I offered.

"I can imagine."

"It was a really dumb thing to do."

"Yes, it was."

I could feel the tears coming. My throat started to choke up. I started to think of the tennis team, and the chance that I'd blown, and how mad Chris was at me, and how disappointed I *knew* Uncle Teddy must be, and how it probably hurt my mom . . .

"I'm really sorry," I managed to say, my voice cracking. "I'll never do anything like it again. I promise."

My mother stepped quickly across the bridge and pulled me close. I hugged her back as hard as I could possibly manage right then. It felt good, just to know that she was there, that she didn't hate me, that it was going to be all right.

"Cally, we all make mistakes. That won't be the last big mistake you make," she said softly in one ear. "What you do is you ask God to forgive you, then pick yourself up and move on."

I suddenly remembered how my mother had held me much like this when I was very young and I'd smashed or careened or wiped out or tripped and stumbled. She'd scoop me up off the ground and hold me until it was safe again, until it was time to run around on my own again.

My mother gave me one more hug, and then returned to her side of the bridge. I found that I could meet her gaze now. The ledger was balanced again, at least with her. I knew she'd forgiven me.

But there was a much larger problem that was not resolved. Without words, we both knew that the time had come for me.

"Mom," I said with as much determination and courage as I could muster, "how do I go about believing in God? How do I do that?"

My mother smiled. "You ask Jesus Christ, who is God's Son, to come into your life."

"But how do I actually *do* that?"

"Well," she said, "it's very hard to believe in God. There are a lot of reasons why it's so hard, but the biggest reason is what the Bible calls sin. When we make mistakes, we feel ashamed and guilty and the last thing in the world we want is for God to look at us just then."

"That makes sense," I said, almost laughing at my dumb mistake now.

"Now, God obviously knows that we're avoiding Him. That's one of the reasons why He sent His Son here. To help us come to know who God is, why He loves us and cares for us . . ."

"But how does that work?" I persisted.

"Think of it like this," my mother said thoughtfully. "When you ask Jesus to come into your life, He enters and begins to teach you how to live a more perfect life. You will always make mistakes, but Jesus will help you see how to avoid making them twice."

"You mean Jesus is a teacher?"

"Yes, among other things," she said, nodding. "There's a nice verse from the Book of Revelation. 'Behold, I stand at the door and knock; if any one hears My voice and opens the door, I will come in to him and eat with him, and he with Me.' "

"So Jesus is a friend too."

"Yes, exactly, among other things," she answered. "But, once He's entered your life, Jesus also serves as the intermediary, the go-between, the person who helps you come to God."

"Intermediary?" I asked, confused.

"Jesus will be someone who talks to God on your behalf. He'll tell God—who is like a judge in a court—that, even though you've made some big mistakes, you're sorry for them and you will trust Jesus to help you learn how to be a better person."

"So Jesus is like your lawyer," I said, remembering the person my mother had talked to recently about a divorce from my father.

"Something like that," she said.

"Jesus is an awful lot of things," I said.

"Yes, He is. But what He is more than anything else is someone who died on a cross for your sins, and was resurrected. He lived again. And if you believe in Jesus, if you ask Him to enter your life, you too will live forever. Does that make sense?"

"Some," I said truthfully. "Actually, more than some."

"And have you made your decision?" she asked, knowing the answer already.

"Yes, I have. I want Jesus to enter my life."

"Then go ahead and ask Him to. I promise He'll answer you."

I did so silently. It was simple, and easy, really. I forgot about myself, just for a moment, and asked Jesus to come into my life. In the twinkling of an eye, the Holy Spirit entered my heart.

The burdens that had seemed so heavy only a moment before now seemed easy to bear. The pain of failure now seemed like a chance to learn from my mistake. The torture of guilt faded into the darkness, replaced by a feeling of acceptance and forgiveness.

It felt like I had gone through my mother's womb a second time, and had been born again.

13

Uncle Teddy really did have an idea, just as he'd promised. It was interesting. Hopeless, but interesting. He came over on the second afternoon of my suspension to talk. He just showed up—unannounced, like he does sometimes—and said he had some details to go over with me.

I was glad he came over. I was going out of my mind with boredom. With all the kids at school—except Timmy, of course, who mostly sleeps during the day—there was almost nothing to do around the house.

As my mother had suggested, I had begun to read through the Gospels pretty carefully. It was interesting. I guess I had had no idea Jesus said all those things. No idea at all. But there's only so much reading a guy can take, no matter how committed or dedicated you are to something.

Once upon a time, I could sit and read for hours. I don't know why. I just could. I once stayed under my covers on a Saturday morning and finished a Dr. Doolittle book. I just stayed there until I'd finished.

But I sure couldn't sit still like that anymore, not on my life. Now it was like I had ants in my pants. If I wasn't up doing something, then I was thinking about it. And even if I was doing something, I was thinking about doing something else after that. It was crazy.

So I was really glad to see Uncle Teddy when he just showed up at the door. Almost glad enough to give him a big hug. But, of course, I hardly ever give anyone hugs, so I just told him to come on in.

"How ya holdin' up?" he asked as he hung up his topcoat.

"Miserably."

Uncle Teddy laughed. It was a nice laugh, an I-know-what-you're-going-through kind of laugh. "I see. It's like that?"

"I'm about to lose my mind I'm so bored," I admitted.

Uncle Teddy slipped out of his suit jacket and slung it over the arm of our couch. For some reason, I noticed just how nice his clothes were. I guess I'd never really noticed before, but he looked sharp, like he had a really important job. Someday, I'd get him to tell me about it.

"OK, here it is," he said. "I'll sponsor you, pay for the entrance fees and the travel. You just have to play your heart out. Is it a deal?"

I looked at him like he was crazy. "What are you talking about?"

"I'm talking about tennis," he said. "And if you play your cards right—if we play our cards right—maybe you'll get the shot at Evan Grant you want so badly."

I still didn't get it. My sponsor? Entrance fees? Travel? "Uncle Teddy, I don't understand. What do you mean, tennis?"

As an answer, he reached over and pulled something from the pocket inside his suit coat. It was a slick flyer, folded once the long way. On the front was a picture of two kids about my age playing tennis. At the top, it read "Come and see us as the Hilton Head Invitational."

"Hmmm," I mumbled, studying the brochure. I could

see what Uncle Teddy's idea was. It was crazy.

"You can't mean . . . ?" I asked finally, after I'd thumbed through the flyer. Uncle Teddy had remained silent while I looked through it and thought about it.

"It's exactly what I mean," he said firmly.

"But it's a lot of money," I said softly.

"So you'll pay me back when you've made your fame and fortune."

I almost giggled. Me, famous? Or rich? That'll be the day. "You might be waiting an awful long time," I said.

Uncle Teddy shrugged. "So I'll wait. Meanwhile, start practicing your serve again, OK? I don't want it to get rusty. The first tournament is in a week and a half, in Fort Myers, on the Gulf Coast of Florida. It's a two-day tournament. It starts a week from this Saturday."

I couldn't believe Uncle Teddy wanted to pay my way to some of the junior tennis tournaments around the country. That's what he meant about sponsoring me. It was expensive. Only rich kids—like Evan Grant—did it. And I certainly wasn't a rich kid. "Uncle Teddy, this is a crummy idea," I pleaded. "This will cost a fortune—"

"Cally, now listen to me," he said, leaning closer. "This is something I want to do. If I want to spend my money this way, then let me. It's my money, to do with as I see fit. Got it?"

I just nodded. What else could I do? "But how am I going to get *into* some of these tournaments? You can't just walk into them, can you?"

Uncle Teddy leaned back again and smiled about as broadly as I'd ever seen him smile. "That's where you come in, kid. And I have faith in you, yes I do. You'll have to earn your way in, play through the qualifiers

in the first three or four. Until you have a name for
yourself."

"So how many matches to get through qualifiers?"

"A lot," he said. "But, don't worry, you'll make it."

I wasn't so sure. But if Uncle Teddy believed I could
do this, then I was willing to give it a shot. Especially
if it meant a chance to come up against Evan Grant
before next year's tryouts.

"So what are we aiming for?" I asked him. "Just to
get into a few tournaments? To get seeded in one?"

"Nope," he winked. "To get to the National Indoor
Championships in Indianapolis this winter. And to
win it all, once we get there."

I decided to look Evan Grant up the day I went back to school. I know, I know. It was a dumb thing to do. But I had to, I really did. It was something I just had to get off my mind.

I wasn't going to punch him in the nose. I felt like doing just that, but I wouldn't.

My mother, of course, had pointed it out to me. Knowing what I *really* wanted to do to Evan Grant when I saw him, she had again pointed out that Jesus said to "Love your enemies."

I'll tell you what. Being a Christian isn't easy. No, it isn't, not at all. I could see that I was going to fall flat on my face quite a few times. I mean, how are you actually supposed to *love* your enemies? How could I ever love Evan Grant after what he'd done to me?

Somewhere, deep inside, I knew that what Jesus said was right, that you had to give up your anger towards both your enemies and the world before you could begin to live in peace with yourself.

Now, that didn't make it any easier for me when I *thought* about facing Evan Grant. I still wanted to stuff him into a locker or something. But, knowing that I was supposed to "do good" to him when I finally did meet him again made the actual burden just a little lighter.

I started looking for him the moment I walked

through the door. I kept an eye on his locker right before homeroom, but he didn't show. Disappointed, I slipped into my own homeroom right before the bell rang.

I fidgeted the whole time. Everyone else in the homeroom was talking away at 100 miles an hour to one or more of their neighbors. But I hadn't really made any friends at Roosevelt yet—not really, not the kind of friends I'd go out of my way to talk to.

So, I just sort of sat in my chair and fumed for the fifteen minutes we were there. I was pretty miserable.

I leaped out of the class almost an instant after the bell rang, and walked as quickly as I could back towards Evan Grant's locker. In fact, I was walking so fast I almost ran over this girl who was turning the corner from another hallway just as I was bolting past.

"Oh, I'm sorry!" this girl gushed as I slammed into her and knocked her books from her hands. Papers flew off in different directions. One of her books made a deep *thunk* when it landed on the floor.

"No, I'm sorry, it was my fault. Really," I said quickly, stooping down to help her gather up her papers. As I began to pick them up, I couldn't help noticing the titles at the top of a group of little booklets that were mixed in with her school books and papers.

The title on one, for instance, was "Is Jesus Who He Said He Was?" Another read, "Is Jesus the Son of God?" Still a third was titled, "Are We Promised Eternal Life?"

As I handed her books and papers back to her, I found myself staring at a big, wooden cross that hung from her neck. It was a pretty big cross. It probably banged around when she ran.

"Thanks!" she said, quickly assembling all the various papers and books into a neat pile and wrapping both arms underneath them, the way girls always do when they're carrying a zillion books between classes. I shifted my own books back under one arm.

"No problem," I mumbled, glancing at that huge cross around her neck again. "It was my fault. Sorry."

She gave me a large, buck-toothed grin. "No, it wasn't. I was in a hurry. I should have watched where I was going."

I shook my head. "No, really. I slammed right into you. I was the one who was in a hurry."

We both just sort of stared at each other for a moment, silently debating over who was at fault. It wasn't awkward, really. Not at all. In fact, it was nice, in a way. Then, almost as if on cue, we both started laughing, more at ourselves than at each other.

"Well, anyway, thanks for helping," she said, glancing up at one of the wall clocks. "I need to get going. I'll be late."

"Yeah, me too."

"See ya around," she said, and began to walk past me.

I'd taken one step when I blurted, "Hey! Can I ask you a question?"

She turned and gave me a curious, expectant look. "Sure. What?"

I glanced down at my shoes for an instant. "What . . . what are all those little booklets about? I mean, I can see that you're wearing that cross, and I was just sort of wondering . . ."

She quickly took a few from the pile and offered them to me. "Here. Would you like to look at some?"

I almost recoiled from them. I'm not sure why. It was a natural reaction. I reached up and ran a hand through my hair to avoid taking them from her. "Well, no, that's OK," I said, almost grimacing. "I was just sort of curious what they were all about, that's all."

She pulled back her offer without hesitation. "Oh, they're just little books that explain who Jesus Christ is. When people ask, it's easier to give them one of these."

"I see," I said, nodding. "So you're . . . a born-again Christian?"

"Yes, I am, praise the Lord," she said, beaming proudly. "I've turned my life over to Christ."

I wondered how she could just say it like that, how she could be so bold about it. "Oh," was all I managed to say in response.

"And you?" she asked, her eyes boring in on me.

I felt profoundly uneasy. I knew I couldn't say "Praise the Lord!" just like that. Maybe I'd never be able to. I don't know. Yet, I knew that I'd become a Christian. I had no doubt about that, none at all.

"Yes, I'm a Christian," I said. "I made the decision a few days ago."

Without warning, this girl shifted all of those books and papers to one arm, leaned over and gave me a quick hug. It took me completely by surprise. "Oh, that's so wonderful!" she said with an exuberance I'd never seen before. "Praise God!"

I said nothing in return, although I did manage to smile grimly and nod to her as she pulled away. "Yeah, it *is* pretty neat," I said. "I've been reading a lot of the Bible in the last couple days."

She dropped to one knee, setting her books down, and pulled out a piece of paper and a pencil. Quickly, she jotted down her name and telephone number. She handed them to me. "My name's Elaine Cimons, with a 'C,' " she said. "We should get together, just to talk."

"Great," I said, nodding again numbly. This girl was like a tornado. She had just spun into my life without

warning, causing my emotions and thoughts to fly off
in different directions. "I . . . I'll give you a call after
school some night."

"And your name is?"

"Oh," I said dimly. "Cally James. My name's Cally
James."

"Well, Cally James," she answered brightly, "now
I'm really gonna be late to class. So I'll talk to ya later,
OK? Give me a call." Then she was gone in an instant,
just like that. Just like a tornado that suddenly bolts
from the ground, off in search of another victim.

I wondered idly who God had planted squarely in
my path, just when I thought it was safe to come back
to school.

*   *   *   *   *

I didn't find Evan Grant until the break between
second and third period. He finally decided to visit his
locker, with his full entourage in tow. There must have
been six or seven other kids with him.

I tried to walk right up to him. No dice. The first of
his many "bodyguards" stepped right in my path.

"I thought you got kicked out of school?" said body-
guard number one.

"Yeah, who let you back in, Deep South?" said number two.

I didn't know either of their names — not that I cared
all that much what they were — so I bore straight in for
Evan Grant without answering. Two others just sort
of sidled in front of me, blocking my path.

"You goin' somewhere?" asked number three.

I cocked my head slightly, acknowledging his pres-
ence. "No, I just want to talk to Evan," I said firmly.

"How come?" asked number four.

This was getting ridiculous. It felt like I was trying
to weave my way through the Secret Service to get to

the President of the United States, for crying out loud.

"I just want to ask him something," I answered, glancing over at Evan Grant, who was still rummaging through his locker for something.

"What's that, exactly?" said number three.

"Evan, can I ask you something?" I said in a louder voice. He still wouldn't turn around.

"I think he's busy," said one of the thugs. I couldn't tell which one. "Why don't ya try later?"

"I think I want to ask him something right now," I persisted.

"Give it up, Deep South," one of the thugs whispered from behind me. "You lost. Big time."

I almost whirled on the guy. But I held my place. He wasn't who I wanted. I wanted Evan Grant.

"Yeah, maybe. But what does it profit a man to gain the whole world and lose his life," I said over my shoulder, paraphrasing something from the Book of Mark my mother had pointed out to me the night before. *That oughta throw him for a loop,* I thought.

"What's that s'posed to mean?" the thug hissed back.

"It means," Evan Grant answered, suddenly turning to face me, "that this *boy* has suddenly found religion, just like all of those Bible-thumpers from down in God's country."

I just shrugged. At least I'd finally gotten his attention. "Yeah, I've accepted Christ," I said quickly, with only a tiny bit of hesitation.

Evan Grant shook his head sadly. "What a cryin' shame," he said dolefully. "Another kid brainwashed."

"It was my own decision," I answered, wondering how the conversation had turned this way without any warning. "And I'm proud of it."

Grant sneered. "Yeah, I'll bet you are. You were

probably so miserable at home you figured you had to pour out your soul to God—"

"I know you were responsible," I said in a low voice, pitching it directly at him. "I know it was you."

"You do, huh?" Grant said through half-lidded eyes that seemed amused, almost pleased, by the conversation. "You're pretty sure of that?"

"Yes, I am," I said. "*Very* sure of that. And I think you're a coward. I think you were afraid to face me."

The thugs all bristled, closing in on me. Evan Grant's eyes smoldered. His lips tightened into a grim smile. "I'm not afraid of you, Deep South," he said, his voice controlled. "You're a joke on the court. You can't touch me."

"Then why'd you send Johnny after me, if you're not afraid?" I said.

Evan Grant laughed. "So who ever said I'd do something like that? You were the numbskull who picked a fight with Johnny, not me."

"You didn't answer my question," I said, pressing on. "Why are you afraid of me?"

Evan Grant finally eased his way through his bodyguards to face me directly. "I'm not afraid of *you* or anyone else," he said, jabbing a finger in my direction. "Got it?"

"I think you are afraid," I answered, looking him directly in the eye. "And we'll meet again. Just the two of us. You can count on that." Then I left.

I ignored their cacophony of taunts in my wake. I had made my point. And I was quite sure Evan Grant had heard it too.

15

Steve Walker told me what to expect at the tournament in Florida. In fact, he drilled it into my head as we practiced nearly every part of my game each night the week before Uncle Teddy and I left.

"You'll probably have two or three qualifying matches by the middle of the afternoon Saturday," he said. "Assuming you get through those, and you will, then you'll play your first seeded match that night. Then I'm sure they'll play the quarters, semis, and finals on Sunday."

"But if I lose the first match?"

"Then you come home and try again the next time."

"And what if I lose the first match *then?*"

"Then you come home and try again the next tournament."

"And if I lose right away again?"

"Then you hope your uncle has deep pockets and try again."

"So when do I give up?"

"You don't."

That's what I liked about Steve. He may have given up on his own career, sort of, but he sure could dole out a big helping of hope and confidence when he wanted to.

"Cally," he said on Thursday night, the day before Uncle Teddy and I were set to climb aboard a 747 for

Florida, "you really only have to remember one thing when you're down there."

"What's that?"

"Serve and volley, serve and volley, serve and volley."

"So I guess I should serve and volley?" I said with a smart-aleck grin. He flicked a tennis ball at me.

"Cally, seriously, your serve has improved immensely in the last couple of months," Steve said. "With your size and quickness, you have the ability to roll right over people, like Boris Becker."

"Yeah, sure," I said frowning. "I'm sure there are zillions of kids out there my age who can plaster me."

Steve shook his head firmly. "No, there aren't, Cally. You'd be surprised. There *aren't* all that many kids out there with your kind of talent, or your drive. It's rare. You just have to decide it's what you want to do and then go out and do it."

I sighed. I'd heard Steve's sermon before. I think I only half-believed it. "So it's really that easy? I just waltz in, take everybody by storm, and waltz out?"

"You know better," he said. "It's not easy. But it can be done."

*   *   *   *   *

My face was glued to the side of the window as we took off from National Airport, which is just across the Potomac River. The airplane made a hard, steep left turn almost immediately after we took off. I stared at all the monuments, fascinated at how they looked from the air.

"It's a beautiful city, isn't it?" Uncle Teddy said.

"Sure is," I mumbled. "It tooks different, somehow."

"It looks that way to me too every time I take off from here," he answered, looking out at the city over my shoulder.

"You know, I've never been on an airplane before," I said to Uncle Teddy without taking my eyes off the city.

"Your mother told me," he said with a slight chuckle. "You scared?"

"Nah," I said. "This is a blast."

"That's what I thought you'd say."

* * * * *

We changed planes in Orlando, and arrived in Fort Myers about 10 P.M. Uncle Teddy seemed to know exactly where to go and what to do. Within a matter of minutes, it seemed, all of our bags were packed in the back of a rented car.

"Are there coconuts at the top of those palm trees?" I asked him as we barreled down a highway.

"Yep, but not many at this time of year," he said.

"Hey, do you know where we're going?" I asked.

"Yep, sure do. A place called Sanibel Island. I've traded for a condo for this weekend. Ever heard of it?"

I shook my head. I'd never heard of a lot of places.

The place was dark when we pulled into a gravel driveway. I climbed into bed without unpacking because I had a 7 A.M. match. Naturally, though, I couldn't get to sleep right away, partly because I was in a new bed, but mostly because I couldn't stop thinking about tomorrow.

It sure cost Uncle Teddy a lot to come down here. What if I get killed the first match? What if I can't get my first serve in? What if I can't return his first serve? What if . . .

The alarm clock pierced through the veil of sleep like a siren, grating against my raw, jangled nerves. I slammed my hand on the snooze button and rolled over, drifting off to sleep again. It had been at least midnight before I'd drifted off to sleep . . .

"Up and at 'em!" Uncle Teddy said brightly as he entered my room and flipped on the light. "Rise and shine! Breakfast's ready."

I groaned. The sun hadn't even come up yet. How could anyone be so cheery at this time of day? "AAArrrggghhh," I grumbled as I pulled the covers over my head.

"If you're not up, dressed, and in the kitchen in the next five minutes, I'm bringing a pan of cold water in here and dumping it on your head," Uncle Teddy warned as he slipped out of the room again.

I'm no dummy. I was in the kitchen in world record time. I tied my Brooks shoes in the kitchen, while I took bites out of the bagel Uncle Teddy had fixed. I made a face at the oatmeal he'd made me, but I ate it without a complaint.

"Now, remember, even in the early matches, you need to drink plenty of water on the court," Uncle Teddy said as we barreled back down the same highway we'd come in on. "If you dehydrate, you'll collapse. So drink, OK?"

I nodded grimly. My palms were ice-cold. I was scared stiff. I hadn't really thought about what I was doing, not really, until this very moment. What in the world was I doing here, in a strange place, on my way to a tennis tournament?

Uncle Teddy reached a hand out and placed it on my shoulder. "You'll do just fine, Cally," he said gently. "Don't worry so much. What is it that Steve's always telling you?"

"Hit out," I answered automatically, like a robot who's been programmed. "Short balls kill you, so hit out and adjust after that."

"There you go," he said reassuringly. "You'll be all right after the first game's under way. I promise."

I have no idea how Uncle Teddy knew where we were going, but I didn't doubt him. He always seemed to know where he was going. In an instant, or so it seemed, we had arrived.

The tennis center was unbelievable. I think it went on forever. There must have been a thousand courts on the grounds. Well, maybe not a thousand, but close. They seemed to stretch off forever in either direction.

We pulled up to the clubhouse and got out. I stared around in awe. I had no idea they had clubs like this around the country. No idea at all.

Uncle Teddy gazed at the board, which contained the draw, for several moments after we'd arrived. I spotted my last name at the bottom, below the sixteen seeds, but I couldn't tell right away what it meant.

"Good," Uncle Teddy said firmly. "If you make it through qualifying, you'll play the first seed right away. That oughta shake 'em up."

"Are you nuts?" I whispered, afraid some of the other kids who were milling around the place would hear me. "Why would I want to play the top seed right away?"

"So that when you beat him, everyone here will know who you are and they'll watch you on Sunday, that's why," he answered.

I just shook my head, wondering if maybe my uncle hadn't lost his marbles. "Well, I gotta get through the first match," I grumbled.

"That you do, kid, that you do," he said.

I was on Court 22—which was in outer Mongolia, no doubt—so we drove around until we spotted it. It was in outer Mongolia.

I pulled my bag from the trunk. Uncle Teddy followed with a bucket of old balls I used to practice serves. My opponent was already on the court, practicing his serve, so I moved over to the court beside him and limbered up with a few booming serves. They were all out by three feet.

I watched my opponent out of the corner of my eye. I'm sure he was doing exactly the same. As I watched him, I could feel the tension start to ease, the fears starting to recede. Shoot, he was just a kid, like me. And he didn't hit all that hard. My first serve was better. I could tell.

Finally, after I'd pulled my serve back to where I was getting it in consistently, I drifted back to the car, where Uncle Teddy had set himself up to watch the match.

He had a cup of coffee in one hand and three newspapers — *The New York Times, The Wall Street Journal,* and *USA Today* — on the other side. He seemed to be all set. I wondered if I was.

"You should be able to jump on his second serve," he told me as I slipped into the seat beside him.

"I know," I said, nodding. "I can see that."

"Well, then, go do it," he said, pulling one of the newspapers in front of him. In a strange sort of way, it gave me a lot of confidence. It was like he *expected* me to be here for a while today, so he was just taking it all in stride. Well, if he could, I figured, then so could I.

I walked out on the court and introduced myself. It's funny, but I think I forgot his name almost from the instant he told it to me. I wasn't paying attention to what his name was, or what he looked like.

The only thing I cared about right then was what his serve looked like, how hard he could hit his forehand, whether he could take his backhand down the line, and whether he was quick enough at the net to get to my passing shots.

As we warmed up, I could tell that he didn't have an overpowering backhand. I could work on that right away. His forehand wasn't going to blow me off the court. And when he took balls at the net, I could see instantly that he didn't react as swiftly as he should have.

The match was over after the first two games. I won the spin of the racket and served first. He barely got his racket on my first two serves.

On the third, he returned the ball short and I followed it in with a driving forehand. He could only manage a poor lob back and I crushed an overhead. On the last serve, I followed my second serve into the net and put away a winner off a pretty decent passing shot.

Then, when he served, I came to the net twice on his second serve and won both points with a volley. I passed him on a third return of serve, and then finished off the game with a blistering crosscourt backhand off of his first serve.

And the match was over. We both knew it. There was no way he was going to take one of my service games — not unless my serve blew up, which it almost never did now, thanks to Steve's patience — and I was returning his serve too easily. The final score was 6-0, 6-2.

"Man, where'd you come from?" he said to me after the match, as we both walked back to the clubhouse. Uncle Teddy followed us in the car.

"Washington, D.C.," I answered.

"No, I mean where'd you *come* from? How come you aren't seeded, the way you play?"

I just shrugged. "I've never played in one of these

things," I said. "This is my first tournament."

He just shook his head. "Well, it won't be your last. That's for sure. Not with that serve and that backhand. Where'd you learn to hit like that anyway?"

I smiled to myself, thinking of the countless hours Steve had worked with me. "I have a great coach."

We shook hands. I forgot to ask him where he was from, but I guess it didn't matter. I'd get better at all of this—really *talking* to my opponents, I mean—when I wasn't so nervous and in awe anymore.

"One down, three to go today," Uncle Teddy said simply as we gazed at the board. My next match was on Court 11, so we headed off.

My second match was very different than the first, but with almost the same result. Final score, 6-2, 6-0. He'd never been able to get his first serve in consistently, and I'd killed him on his second serve.

My third match, my last qualifying round, was almost as easy. I lost my serve once, but I broke his about every other time and won 6-3, 6-2.

Uncle Teddy took me to Mac's for lunch, which I inhaled. I was pretty tired, but the matches had been easy enough that I felt like I'd have enough energy to at least give my next opponent—the top seed—a good match later that night.

"You'll do better than that," he said between bites. "I watched him warm up while you were playing that last guy."

"You did?"

"Sure. He was out practicing with a buddy on center court while you were playing. He's got a great first serve, probably as good as yours, but not a whole lot else. He probably skates by with that in most matches. You'll just have to wait for your chances on his second serve."

I nodded silently. I actually like playing guys like that. There were always a lot of fireworks. It was fun. Plus, a match like that wouldn't take a whole lot out of me, which was really important right now.

Two hours and a short nap later, I walked onto center court. There were stands on all four sides, though almost no one was watching. Which didn't surprise me. I mean, I was a nobody and this guy was supposed to mop me up and move into the quarterfinals.

I could see just a hint of surprise in his eyes as he watched me serve. I'd already expected a booming serve from him, so I didn't even flinch as his whizzed past me.

As usual, my uncle had been dead on target. He had a great first serve, and not much else. The match was quick, very quick. It was over in a hurry. He never broke my serve. And I broke his twice, once in the first set and once in the second. Final score, 7-5, 6-4.

"Hey, who are you?" he asked me, clearly very, very angry at himself for losing and at me for coming out of nowhere to beat him.

"Nobody," I said. "Nobody at all."

"Not for long, you won't be," he said grimly. "After this tournament, you'll be on the map. You won't get away with this again."

"Get away with what?" I asked, genuinely perplexed.

"Sneaking up on people," he said, breaking away to go receive his consolations from a group of well-wishers who'd accompanied him.

That stopped me for a moment. Sneaking up on people? All I'd done was come down here to play tennis, nothing else. What was he talking about?

"Don't worry about it," Uncle Teddy said as we barreled down the highway for the third time in two days. "He was just mad. You came at him from no-where. He was expecting an easy match against a qualifier, and he got you instead."

"But what did he mean about sneaking up on him?"

"You were unseeded, and you probably should not have been, that's all. But, he's right, that'll change. After this tournament, I may be able to seed you in almost any tournament I look at. Except the National Indoors, but we'll cross that bridge when we get there."

I just nodded. My eyes were already closed. I was asleep by the time we arrived at the doorstep. Tomorrow would take care of itself.

16

The trophy was tiny. I placed it very carefully right next to the trophies I'd gotten for winning the Birmingham city championships.

I told no one at school about it. The tournament, I mean. I caught a few sidelong glances, and maybe a quizzical look, from Evan Grant. Perhaps he'd seen my name—it *had* been on page 272 of *Tennis* magazine, at the bottom of one of the box scores from the USTA-sanctioned tournaments.

More likely, though, he'd heard about what I'd done through the grapevine. The rich kids' grapevine. One of his pals from somewhere else probably said, Hey, who's this new kid from your neck of the woods?

I can just hear Grant laughing to himself as he tells this pal what a loser, what a nobody, I am. Don't worry, he probably told his pal. This kid's nobody to worry about. He's not really part of our "crowd."

But, of course, that's just Evan Grant's opinion, Uncle Teddy would say. Cally's not a nobody. He may not be rich, and he may not have been born with social graces. But he can acquire those, if he has to.

Me, I wasn't worried. There's a part of the Bible that talks about choices, about who you're going to serve—God or "mammon."

"What's mammon?" I asked my mother one night.

My mother looked up from her Bible. We were down

in the kitchen, after Timmy was in bed for the night. The other kids were downstairs, watching TV. We'd started our own little Bible study, just the two of us.

I love that passage, the one that says where two or more Christians are gathered together, God is there too. "For where two or three are gathered in My name, there am I in the midst of them."

And we were gathered, my mother and I. It didn't matter if no one else was there. We were enough. Just the two of us. *"Mammon* can mean great wealth, or riches," my mother answered. "It can also mean worldly gain."

"Worldly gain?"

My mother smiled. I think she genuinely loved teaching me this stuff. "It means being fabulously successful. Like making so much money you can buy palaces, or becoming a famous movie star."

"Or winning the National Indoors?" I asked, wincing.

"Well, yes," she answered. "But, Cally, remember what that passage says. It isn't winning a championship—even one that big—that's bad—"

"Then what is?" I asked quickly.

"Serving mammon is what's evil," she answered. "Making that goal your god is what's bad. Let's look it up," she said, flipping through the pages of her Bible. "I think it's in the middle of Luke."

We raced to find the passage. It was a game with us. She would tell me, generally, where a story was. Then we'd race through the Bible to see who found it first. She almost always won, but I was getting better.

"OK, it's in Luke, chapter 16—"

"I see it," I said quickly. "Verse 13."

"All right, Ace, then you read it," she laughed.

I read from the soft, leather Bible my mother had

given me. " 'No servant can serve two masters; for either he will hate the one and love the other, or he will be devoted to the one and despise the other. You cannot serve God and mammon.' "

"Do you see it?" she asked.

"See what?"

"The choice you have to make. You have to serve one or the other, God or mammon. You can't serve both."

I glanced back down at the passage. "So if I get in a tough spot, where I have to choose between one or the other . . ."

"Then you must choose God," she said. "But it's really something you have to do all the time, not just at certain points in your life." I wondered, just a little, about Evan Grant. I guess I didn't have any real doubt about who he served. At least right now. "Cally, don't worry about it quite so much. I think you know which of those two you're serving."

"Yeah, it's not as if I'm gonna be rich or famous," I snorted.

"I wouldn't be so sure of that," she said softly. "But I think you can handle it, if you ever are."

Again, I thought of Evan Grant. I couldn't get him out of my mind. Could he handle it, all that money his folks had? I doubted it. I'm not sure I'd be able to. And with all his success in tennis, well . . .

"You know, I sort of hope I never have to find out," I said.

"That would certainly make it easier," my mother answered. "But you've never been one to take the easy path, Cally. You like it where the brambles and the thorns are."

Uncle Teddy entered me in three more tournaments, all of them on indoor courts, in Pennsylvania, New Jersey, and Virginia. They weren't real big ones, with kids who were ranked.

In fact, I didn't come up against a single kid who was ranked in the top 50 nationally. I think Uncle Teddy must have had a reason for this, although I couldn't figure it.

I won all three tournaments, easily. I was starting to think—maybe, just maybe—that I could play with some of those kids, the ones I read about in the magazines. The rising stars, the ones who would take the tennis world by storm when they were older.

Would I be one of those? Did I have what it took? I don't know. But the glimmer of a possibility was beginning to peek around the corner.

I was ranked now, somewhere on the computer. After the last tournament, Uncle Teddy found out, somehow, that I'd finally made it into the top 300 in the U.S. in my age bracket. I guess that meant something.

"It means," Uncle Teddy told me, "that you can go to the qualifying at the National Indoor Championships. The top 100 get in automatically. The other 200 or so have to face each other in the qualifying to make it into the last 28 places. . . ."

"You mean 200 kids fight it out for 28 spots in the

tournament?" I asked, incredulous.

"It's not so hard to figure," Uncle Teddy said. "If 224 kids start in qualifying, after three rounds, there are 28 left. There are 112 after the first, 56 after the second, and 28 after the third."

"And then you have all those rounds in the tournament itself," I said, shaking my head sadly. "I'll never make it, not in a million years."

"Don't give up before you even begin, kid," Uncle Teddy said. "Just take it a match at a time. Remember, once you've made it into the tournament—"

"*If* I make it," I interjected.

"*Once* you've made it in," he answered firmly, "you only play three matches to get to the round of 'Sweet 16.' And there are just three more after that to the finals."

My uncle really kills me sometimes. He made it all seem so easy. When you added it all up, you had to win three matches just to get in, and then seven to make it to the top of the mountain. No way. It was an impossible task.

"If you say so," I sighed.

"You just show up and play, Cally," Uncle Teddy said. "You let me do the worrying. Deal?"

"OK, it's a deal," I said, shrugging. "I'll be there."

"They won't know what hit 'em," Uncle Teddy said.

I didn't say anything. I had this funny thought. I was wondering what it felt like when you were going a zillion miles an hour and you crashed into a brick wall. I guess it probably would hurt. Oh well.

18

Well, here I am, after all. Mom said the whole family needed a Christmas vacation, we only had one other aunt besides Franny, and it didn't cost all that much to pack the kids up and drive to Indianapolis, all things considered.

She *did* promise that everybody would at least wait to see if I actually made it through the qualifying rounds before they showed up to cheer me on. I cringed at the thought. My own cheering section? Ouch.

So on the first day of qualifying—which began the week after Christmas—Aunt Tildy took them all on a tour of greater Indianapolis. Only Chris really complained. He wanted to come see even the first match.

I'm not sure why, but Karen seemed strangely silent. As if she were waiting for the phone to ring. I almost asked her what was up. But, right at the moment, I didn't have the heart for it. My mind was elsewhere.

Jana, John, and Susan were having the time of their lives. Jana, like she will sometimes, was playing games with both of them, first Monopoly, then Life, then Clue, then . . .

And Timmy just watched, like always. He was about ready to walk, even though he'd only just turned six months old. He was already starting to pull up on chairs and tables, so I knew he'd walk early like the rest of the kids.

*　　*　　*　　*　　*

I didn't really think much about Evan Grant. Really. I thought about him only enough to remember that Uncle Teddy had said he was seeded fourth. Fourth in the national championship. Fourth in the whole country.

I was on the other side of the draw, so if I was going to face him it would be in the finals. Fat chance. So I stopped thinking about it. I just wanted to get through qualifying. I'd worry about Evan Grant later.

They say that Indianapolis is the center of the universe for amateur sports. I believe it. The tennis complex alone was fabulous. I felt like I could get lost behind all those green curtains behind the courts.

As he had at the other tournaments, Uncle Teddy stayed with me until I was on the court, then he just sort of faded into the background.

It was hard to pay any attention to him in an indoor facility anyway. The spectators had to watch the matches from behind a huge, soundproofed plate glass window high up above all the courts.

For some reason, I wasn't nearly as nervous as I'd thought I'd be. I think it was the tournaments under my belt, the ones I'd won, that did the trick. Even if they were only small tournaments, it helped.

Plus, I recognized at least a few of the kids from those tournaments. It wasn't as if this whole thing was *brand* new to me.

"Hey, Cally, how ya doin'!" a voice boomed from behind me.

I whirled to see a big, burly kid with sandy blond hair facing me. I couldn't remember his name, not to save my life, but I remembered playing him at the tournament in New Jersey. He'd only taken two games off me.

"Hey," I said lamely. "Long time no see."

He just grinned. Apparently, he didn't hold a grudge against me for the shellacking I'd handed him just a couple of weeks before. "So, you seeded?"

"Nah," I said. "I'm in the qualifying."

He just shook his head sadly and sighed. "Well, there goes one of the twenty-eight spots."

"I wouldn't count on it," I cautioned.

"I would," he said, turning to look up at the clock. "Hey, I gotta go. My match starts in five minutes. See ya around."

"Yeah, see ya," I called out to him as he raced off.

My first match didn't start right away, so, after a few practice serves to stay limber, I drifted up to the spectators' box to watch the first matches.

There were all sorts of kids here. All ages, all sizes and shapes. They were holding the 14s, 16s, and 18s here as well, so it was almost impossible to tell who was what. I just bought a Coke and plopped down in one of the sofas to watch.

Kids, most of them with their parents, buzzed around everywhere. Most of them seemed absolutely thrilled just to be here. They were here, for the national championship. Never mind that they didn't have a chance in the world of winning it. That wasn't what mattered.

So what did matter about it? Winning? Just being here? Just trying your best? I don't know. I'm not sure. I couldn't figure it out to save my life.

My palms started to get cold and clammy as the hour of my first match began to arrive. Uncle Teddy stopped by, briefly, to remind me. As if I needed reminding.

"Relax, kid," he said, mussing my hair a little. "Remember to hit out and you'll do just fine."

I just grimaced and started to move towards the courts . . .

You know, it's funny. When something is over, you stop worrying about it. That makes sense, doesn't it?

Here I'd been worrying for weeks about the qualifying round, and it wasn't even hard. I breezed through all three of my matches. My opponents took a grand total of nine games from me in the six sets I won.

So I'd attained my goal, sort of. I'd made it into the tournament. But now, for some strange reason, I still wasn't satisfied.

"It's because you want to win the whole thing," Chris said that night in our darkened bedroom in Aunt Tildy's musty basement.

"Come on, get real," I said from my own bed, where I couldn't sleep, even though I was dead tired.

"I am. You can win it. I know you can."

"There are 127 kids who say I can't."

"After tomorrow, there will only be fifteen in your way."

I laughed. "In your dreams. I'll get knocked off in the first or second round."

"No way. You'll see." And to settle it, Chris rolled over and slammed a pillow on top of his head so he couldn't hear my protests.

20

I finally lost my first set. But I guess I shouldn't complain. My first two matches that day had been almost painless. Neither of my opponents in the first and second rounds had much of a first serve, which made it a whole lot easier for me.

All that was forgotten now. Maybe it was the fact that I was facing a seeded player, or that I'd made it to the third round. I don't know. All I *do* know is that my serve had vanished like a thief in the night.

I double-faulted the first set away. Badly. I wasn't even close. My first serves were careening a good two feet beyond the service line.

So I readjusted. My opponent, the ninth seed in the tournament, had a pretty decent return of serve anyway, so I just started to lay back in the second set. We had long rallies, some of them very long. But I decided to be patient, for a change, and see if my game came back.

It did, somewhere towards the end of that second set, when I finally broke his serve and I was serving for the set. One minute my game was gone, then it was back. Very strange, but I wasn't about to complain.

I broke him twice in the third set and he didn't touch my serve. Game, set, and match. And I was in the round of "Sweet 16."

* * * * *

We all had a late pizza, at one of those places where they have games and kids are always wiping out or smashing into each other.

I was so tired now I could hardly move. But I was pretty sure I'd be OK. I could sleep in the next morning, and my first match wasn't until after lunch. So I gorged on pizza and didn't say much.

Karen waited until there were only two of us at the table. Well, three of us, really. Timmy was quietly gnawing on some pizza crust. Everybody else, Mom and Uncle Teddy included, were over at the video games. Karen had hung back with me for some reason.

"Dad called today," she said simply. "I talked to him, at Aunt Tildy's house."

My jaw dropped, in mid-bite. "How did he . . . ?"

"He said he talked to Aunt Franny. She told him we came here for a vacation." Karen was watching me like a hawk, wondering how I'd react.

I tried to be calm. "Does he know about me, about this tournament?"

Karen just nodded. We sat there for a long time, the two of us, not saying anything. It had been a long time. I'd almost forgotten I had a father.

Almost, but not quite. I will never forget. Never. Not as long as I live, no matter what.

Karen tilted her head slightly. "He said he might show up," she said.

"Show up?"

"Here. In Indianapolis."

"When?"

"Tomorrow, or maybe the next day."

The anger started to well up from somewhere very, very deep within me. He wouldn't, he couldn't. He had no right, none at all. When I could think again, it took all my strength just to unclench my teeth.

"Does anyone else know?" I almost growled.

"No, and he asked me not to tell anyone," Karen said, still watching me anxiously. I'm not sure what she *really* thought about our father. I wasn't sure at all about it. I wondered if even she knew herself.

"But why?" I pleaded with Karen. "I don't get it. Why now?"

"I think he wants to see you," Karen answered. "That's what he said."

The words hit me like a jackhammer. *Yeah, I'll just bet he wants to see me.* I suddenly had this very sick feeling in the pit of my stomach.

It was horrible, that feeling. It was hate, and anger, and dread, all mixed up together. I wanted to hit my father and run away from him all at the same time. *Why now? Why right now? Why couldn't he have waited for another time and place?*

"Don't let him come near me, Karen," I said finally. "I mean it. I don't want to see him until the tournament's over. Do you hear me? I just don't want to see him."

Karen nodded again. I think she understood. At least I hoped she did.

I closed my eyes for a second and prayed. I hadn't done that very much, but I had no choice. I was so angry I couldn't even see straight. Left on my own, I'd hate my father forever.

But I didn't want to do that. One of the Ten Commandments is that you're supposed to honor your parents. Well, I surely honored my mother. She was the best. It was easy to honor her. But honor my father, the worm?

"God," I prayed silently, "I don't know how to do

that. I really don't. I know I'm supposed to, but I don't
think I can. Please help me. I can't do this. I just
can't." Then, I ended the prayer as my mother had
taught me. "I ask this in the name of Jesus Christ.
Amen."

I looked up, then. Karen was staring at me like I'd
lost my mind. She didn't say anything. I just smiled,
and shrugged. A peaceful calm had come over me,
along with the knowledge that I could face my father,
and the relief from that burden was almost overwhelming.

"Don't hate him, Cally," Karen pleaded.

"I'm trying not to," I answered truthfully. "I really
am."

I'm not really sure how I made it through the round of 16 and then the quarterfinals the next day, but I did. I kept one eye on the court and another on the plate glass window high up above the courts to see if my father ever showed up.

Somehow I managed to win both of those matches. In the first, I just served and volleyed, served and volleyed, and served and volleyed. I was sure my opponent was sick and tired of seeing me at the net. I was there almost constantly.

He tried everything to keep me away, but it was futile. I was so angry inside, still, that I smashed into oblivion every lob he sent up. And I put his passing shots away with a viciousness that surprised me.

I was lucky in the second match. According to the draw, I should have faced the second seed in the tournament. But he'd been bumped off earlier in the tournament by an "unknown"—just like me—and I found myself facing a plucky, but unseeded, opponent.

It turned out to be the tightest match I'd had so far. We went to a tiebreaker in the first set when neither of us lost our serve. I won the tiebreaker with two blistering returns of his first serve, first a forehand down the line and then a scorching crosscourt backhand that dipped under his racket as he rushed the net.

In the second set, I didn't break his serve until the 11th game of the set. I held my serve to win, 7-5.

My father never showed, at least not that I could see. I did finally stop looking for him during the tie-breaker of the second match.

Meanwhile, Karen was keeping her eyes peeled for him as well. I'd managed to keep the family from showing up for my earlier rounds, but there was no way I was going to keep them away today.

Susan kept her nose plastered against the plate glass window the entire time I was on the courts. Chris kept his eyes glued on my matches as well. So did John, by and large. Karen split her time between my match and the doorways. Jana watched the older boys playing other matches.

Karen and I had decided late the night before not to tell Mom that our father was thinking about "showing up." We both figured that she had enough to worry about.

As we all drove home that night in Aunt Tildy's car, I found myself thinking about how weird things get sometimes, how the world is never quite like you think it ought to be.

Here I was, just a step away from playing for a national championship, and I was more worried about whether my father would show up for the match than I was who my opponent might be.

Part of me felt like there was justice in there some-how, that you were supposed to worry more about whether your father really loved you and *not* whether you were going to win a national tennis champion-ship.

But the other part of me thought it was really unfair that my bum of a father should have forced me to make a choice between the two in the first place.

It was strange, but I hadn't really paid much attention to what Evan Grant was doing in the tournament. I'd seen his name on the board, but I hadn't really watched his progression.

I paid attention now, though. We were both in the semifinals. He was about to face the number one seed in the tournament, while I was set to go up against the third seed. If we both won, well . . .

I was quite sure Evan Grant had watched my progression. I was even more sure of that when he wouldn't even look at me when our paths crossed for the first time on the courts. His match was right next to mine.

I lost the first set of my match because I was spending as much time watching Evan Grant as I was my own opponent. In between points in my match, I kept glancing over to see how he was doing. I know I shouldn't have, but I couldn't help myself.

That stopped, though, as soon as I realized that I was about to let the match slip away. I was careless with points. I wasn't following balls to the net when I should have. I double-faulted at crucial times because I wasn't concentrating.

In between sets, as we changed sides, I slammed my racket down so hard I almost broke it.

"Hey, Deep South, I wouldn't do that," Evan Grant's

nasal voice said from behind me. "You break that racket, you'll have to use that cheapo replacement you always carry around with you."

I could almost hear Steve's sharp rebuke in my mind. Never let 'em see that you're angry or nervous. It'll kill you, he would say. Don't let your emotions run your game, let your shots run it. Let the months of practice sharpening your skill run the game.

Easier said than done, Steve, I thought. But I would try. I really would. I'd give it my best shot.

I took a deep breath and glanced up at the spectators before I served to start the second set. My family was gathered there, watching anxiously. Chris was pacing. Susan still had her nose plastered against the window.

Uncle Teddy, though, was doing something rather strange, for him. He was swinging an imaginary racket through the air. Over and over, he kept swinging an imaginary backhand. Then he would point at my opponent. Imaginary backhand, then point.

Finally, it dawned on me. I understood what he was trying to tell me. Work on his backhand, Uncle Teddy was telling me. That was his weakness, his Achilles heel. I glanced back up at Uncle Teddy and nodded silently. My uncle smiled broadly.

It turned the tide almost instantly. I held my serve easily, then I drove everything deep to his backhand in the second game of the set.

Backhand to backhand, I was going to come out on top. I was very sure of my own backhand, and I could hit it deep with regular precision. He couldn't, and that was the difference in the match. I broke him in the second game, and then again in the fourth.

While he tried to adjust, to keep me from pinning him deep in the corner on his own backhand, the third set was almost a repeat of the second. He just couldn't get around the fact that his backhand was a liability. I ended up winning the match going away.

It was funny, but I could hear the muffled yells from behind the plate glass window when I won the last point of the match. My family must really have been yelling loud for me to hear it down on the court. They probably scared everybody in the place.

I glanced up, and Chris was hopping around like a Mexican jumping bean. Uncle Teddy was hugging my mother. I walked to the net, grim-faced, and shook hands with my crestfallen opponent, who barely looked at me.

I heard the voice right after that. The voice. The one I hadn't heard in almost a year, the one I really never wanted to hear again, maybe for the rest of my life.

It came at me from behind the heavy green curtain that surrounded the courts, a soft, pleading voice that brought back every bad memory I'd blocked from my mind since we'd moved to Washington.

"Cally," my father called out. "Can I talk to you for a second?"

Feeling a sudden, crushing weight on my shoulders, I turned slowly. My father was standing deep in the shadows behind the court, in a place where only I could see him. I couldn't even imagine how he'd gotten there. I was too shocked to think about it.

"Cally, can I talk to you," my father asked again.

I started walking numbly in his direction. As I drew near, I could see that he'd changed. A lot.

His face was almost gaunt. He'd lost even more hair. I could see the mottled spots from his scalp showing through the thin strands of hair that he combed over the top. His arms looked almost skinny, especially beside the beer belly that now protruded much further than it ever had before.

I couldn't help myself. I felt sick just looking at him. I wanted to run away, to hide. I didn't want to talk to him, not now, not ever. There was nothing he could say to me that would ever make it right.

He kept his hands in his pockets as I approached. There would be no warm embrace, no joyful reunion. No way. I think he knew that.

"Cally, boy, have you changed," he said when I was within earshot. "You're not the same kid I knew in Birmingham. You've almost grown up."

"Yeah, well, things change," I somehow managed to say through the handful of emotions that were threatening to close off my windpipe.

"Amen, boy, they sure do," he drawled.

"Why did you come here?" I asked suddenly, no longer able to contain my anger. "Why?"

He ignored my question. "I hear tell you became a Christian," he said instead. "That right? Your momma get to you finally?"

I almost rushed at him. I'm not sure why I didn't. I think it was this strange sense of peaceful calm that was beginning to come over me that held me back. It came from nowhere, and everywhere, all at once.

"Yes, sir, I've become a Christian," I answered. "And Mom and I do talk about it all the time."

"Yeah, I can imagine," he said with a sneer almost forming at the corners of his mouth. "Well, anyway, water over the bridge—"

"Under the bridge," I said, correcting him.

"Yeah, that too," he said quickly, flashing me a wide grin. Then, without warning, he turned his head and spat. An ugly, green hawker landed at the base of the wall and slowly worked its way toward the floor.

"Dad, that's gross," I said.

"Ah, ain't nobody gonna see it back here," he said. "So hush, boy. Don't speak to your poppa like that."

I think it was right then, at that moment, that it finally dawned on me. He was drunk. Not out of his mind, like he got sometimes, but still pretty drunk. He'd probably been downing beers in the car on the drive up to Indianapolis. I shuddered at the thought.

I wanted to get out of the shadows, away from him. Perhaps sensing this, he reached out and grabbed me by the arm. It hurt like crazy, but I didn't say anything or try to squirm away. I just stood there, waiting.

"I'm comin' back," he whispered. I could smell the booze on his breath, now that I was closer. "You tell your momma that I still love her, and that I wanna come back." He was almost wild-eyed, crazy out of his mind. "You tell her, Cally, OK? She trusts you."

"Dad, I don't think . . ."

"Hush!" he almost hissed, gripping my arm even tighter. "Just tell her, boy. I mean it. You tell her that I love her and that I wanna come back. OK?"

I looked my father in the eye, blocking the pain I was now feeling in my right arm, the one I served and played with. He could only face my gaze for a moment before he was compelled to look away. "OK, Dad, sure I'll tell her. If that's what you want, I'll tell her."

"That's all I ask," he said, relaxing his grip. "She don't have to forgive me, least not now. We can talk about that later."

Then he was gone, like some wraith that fades into the darkness when the lights come on. I gave silent thanks to the Lord for holding me up, because I could not have faced him otherwise.

What haunted my father was too strong, too powerful. I knew I could not have faced him, or it, alone. Only God can chase it away. I knew that, now.

23

There was no entourage around him, now. No
bodyguards or pals to prop him up. It was just the two
of us, alone, on a court in the middle of Indianapolis,
Indiana, playing for a national championship.

Nearly all of the kids who'd come to the tennis complex with such high hopes had now gone home, their
dreams of winning the National Indoors back on the
shelf until next year. Only two dreams were still alive.

My mother had suggested I put the match, and the
outcome, in God's hands. Gladly, I'd said. I would play
my heart out to win. I meant to put up a fierce, coura-
geous, and fearless battle. The outcome would then
take care of itself.

I had told only Karen about my encounter with our
father in the shadows behind the tennis courts. I decided that I'd wait until later to fulfill my promise to
my father.

Karen had been bitterly disappointed that he had
not tried to see her as well, but she calmed down
when I'd explained that it would have been impossible with Mom, Uncle Teddy, and all the kids around.
She didn't like it, but she agreed it made sense.

I'd warmed up with Chris before the match, earlier
in the day. Chris was so excited he was hitting everything back at me as hard as he could. I told him if he
didn't calm down, he'd break the strings on his racket.

It was a strange feeling, walking onto the court to face Evan Grant. There was only one spectator near-by, a court monitor who would sit up in the chair as a referee of sorts during the match.

It almost didn't seem real. It seemed like just anoth-er match. Only it *wasn't* just another match. It was against Evan Grant, for a national championship. Still, I was having a hard time convincing myself of that.

I arrived at the court first and hit a few serves while I waited. When Evan Grant finally arrived, I couldn't help but notice that he was decked out in a very ex-pensive, jet-black warm-up suit. I knew how expen-sive it was because we sold one back at the club in Washington.

He was carrying a whole bunch of rackets in an oversized bag. I glanced over at the lone spare I always brought to matches, an old racket I had bought years ago.

When he shucked his warm-ups, it looked as if his tennis clothes had been dry-cleaned. I smiled to my-self as I remembered Susan, rag in hand, cleaning the tar off my Brooks shoes and my mother double-stitch-ing my white shorts.

He didn't say a word. But, then, I hadn't expected him to. But his coldness, his aloofness, didn't bother me. Not now, not anymore.

I pulled a new, fuzzy yellow ball from one of my pockets and held it up so he could see it. Evan nodded almost imperceptibly. With a graceful, practiced ease I dropped it from the sky and hit a looping practice volley across the net towards him. It had begun.

Evan returned it crisply. But he didn't return it to the middle of the court, as you always do during warm-ups. Instead, he hit a sharp, crosscourt forehand that I had to really stretch to get to. I didn't get much on the return, which he put away with an angled backhand.

He quickly pulled a ball from his pocket and shot it across the net to me. I almost returned the ball as he had, but decided against it. He could play those mind games. I didn't want to. I just wanted to beat him.

We almost played a match during the warm-ups. Evan was working every angle, trying to intimidate me. But it wasn't going to work today, not on the court. He'd have to do more than talk and bluster to beat me. I would make sure of that.

When we came to the center for the racket spin, he finally decided to speak to me. "You might as well give up, Deep South," he said under his breath so only I could hear. "You're not in my league and you know it. You don't have a prayer."

I just smiled back at him. No reply was necessary, really. As Steve said, I'd let my racket do the talking. And he was wrong anyway, of course. I did have a prayer.

He won the spin and decided to serve first. As he took his warm-ups, I was mildly surprised by his serves. They were precise, carefully angled serves. But there wasn't the force behind them that I'd expected. I knew I'd be able to return them.

In fact, I teed off on his very first serve. I guessed right that he'd carry it wide. I moved over two paces as the ball was in air and cracked the return down the line. It just caught the outside line, deep, and whizzed past Evan. I'd drawn the first blood.

He crossed me up on his next two serves, though, and won the points easily after a series of volleys. I was impressed. Once he had an advantage during a point, he pressed and pressed until you either made a mistake or gave him a shot he could crunch.

Which meant I had to make sure he didn't keep me off balance. I had to hit deep, even if that meant some of the balls carried long. On his fourth serve, I hit it too deep. I brought the ball back inside the back line on my return of his fifth serve, but he still won the point when he took it on the short hop, rushed the net, and put away my attempt at a lob.

Evan was grinning from ear to ear when we changed sides. "I tried to warn you," he said smugly. "You're not in my league, Deep South."

I still didn't say anything and crossed to the other side. He'd have to return my serves, now, and I was genuinely curious to see how he'd handle them.

I didn't get my first serve in on the first two points, and Evan rushed the net behind both of my second serves. They were pretty decent second serves, but he still won both points at the net. He won both points. His grin was so wide, he looked like a Cheshire cat.

But then I hit four blazing serves in a row. I can do that sometimes, when I'm really on my game. None of them were aces, but Evan never really got his racket on any of them. Two of his returns drifted wide, and I put the other two away for easy winners. My game.

The third game was a long one. He really struggled to hold his serve. We had two very long rallies at deuce points, both of which he won when I hit balls too deep. Although he won the game, the Cheshire grin and smart-aleck remarks were now gone as we changed sides.

I won my serve in the fourth game without much problem. He only returned one serve with any authority, and I still won the point with a stretching drop shot at the net. I noticed a fleeting flash of disappointment cross Evan's face.

It was inevitable, really. At least it seemed so to me. I broke Evan in the fifth game of the set by following two of his serves to the net, and with two hard returns on first serves, one with a crosscourt backhand and the other with a down-the-line forehand.

Evan Grant's jaw was so tight as we changed sides after the fifth game I wondered if maybe he was going to hurt himself.

He changed strategy instantly. Instead of trying to return my first serves hard, he either returned with a high, looping lob or he cut it so that it just dropped over the net as I rushed in. Either one was tough to return and I struggled for the first time to hold my serve.

And he changed his serve as well, hitting biting, twisting serves that popped up off the indoor carpet in funny directions. Those kinds of serves were slower, but more difficult to return with precision. He held his serve easily, maintaining control of each point.

The first set ended not with a bang but a whimper. Despite valiant efforts by Evan to move me around the court, I was getting my first serves in and he was having a very difficult time keeping me away from the net. I won the eighth and tenth games and took the first set.

I could see, however, that the gears were spinning furiously in Evan Grant's mind as we rested for a moment between sets. I knew he would change strategy for a third time, at least when I was serving, and I wasn't disappointed.

After holding his serve in the first game of the second set, he moved up three steps, well inside the baseline, and took my first serves just as they came up off the carpet.

It was harder to do, but he successfully returned

two of my serves for clear winners and returned two more deep enough to give himself an advantage. He finally broke my serve, forcing me to change my strategy.

Which I did on my next serve. I still put plenty of zip on the serves, but I angled them more, which made it tough, if not impossible, for Evan to return with any force. All he could do was stick his racket out if the ball landed within the stripes. I held my serve.

Evan Grant's confidence and cockiness had returned, though, and he held his own serve for the rest of the second set. It too ended rather unceremoniously on a fairly routine overhead by Grant for a winner.

We were tied at one set apiece and I had a feeling that the third, and final, set was going to be a doozy, one that we'd both remember for awhile. It was almost as if the first two sets had been a test, just to see if we were both worthy opponents.

"That first set was pure luck," he growled at me in between sets. "I'm gonna crush you now."

I broke Steve's law and answered the taunt. "I don't think so," I said simply.

"Oh, I *know* so," he said with that maddeningly cocky grin. "You have no right to be on this court."

"Sure I do," I answered. "I have every right—"

"You're not even in my league. You're lucky to be here."

I glanced down at his bag, which must have cost a small fortune just by itself. A dozen very expensive rackets were piled inside it, along with a first-class Gortex warm-up. His shoes were brand-new, as were his shirt and pants. And he had a fresh, new shirt inside the bag, which he was changing into. I couldn't help thinking that maybe he was right. I really wasn't in his league.

"Maybe I am lucky," I said finally. "But I know one thing."

"Yeah, and what's that, Deep South?" he answered.

"I'm better than you, and you know it," I said, grabbing my racket and heading back out on the court.

"You'll have to prove it," Evan Grant shouted.

"I will," I said, more to myself than to him.

I was glad I was serving to start the final set. I decided to move the pace up a notch, just to see what happened. Grant had moved back beyond the baseline, very deep. His back was almost against the curtain at the back of the court. It would be hard to ace him.

My first serve boomed deep into his forehand side. Because he was standing so deep, he was able to get his racket on it. I took the half-volley at mid-court and sent it back to his backhand side. Grant was already moving that way and sent a backhand whistling down the line.

But I had anticipated his shot. I stepped up to the net, let the ball crack into my racket just as it crossed the net, and sent it back sharply to his forehand side for a winner.

Grant just glowered at me, steam practically coming out of his ears. I was pretty sure no one ever did things like that to him.

We traded points from that point until it was 40-deuce. Standing deep allowed Grant to stay in each point, assuming he could get to my serve, which he almost always could.

On the deuce serve, I decided not to come to the net. We rallied for a long time, each of us trying to push the other into a corner. My backhand kept me in the point time after time. I finally took a chance and hit a heavy topspin backhand deep to his backhand and rushed the net.

Grant hit a high, arcing lob to my backhand side. I reacted quickly, moving to the side to take it with an angled overhead. I cracked it as hard as I could. The ball jumped off my racket. I could see it land just inside the line on the other side for a clear winner.

"Out!" Evan bellowed, holding one forefinger up in the traditional sign indicating he felt the ball had carried long.

I just stood there in shock for a moment. I couldn't believe he was deliberately cheating, on such a crucial point. The ball had been in by several inches.

I looked up at the court monitor for help. He just shrugged. "He was in a better position to see it," the monitor said. "I can't overrule him, even if I wanted to."

"But the ball was in," I protested, ignoring Grant for the moment. "You saw it—"

"Sure, it looked good to me," he said, clearly taking my side. "But it's his call."

"Hey!" Grant yelled at the monitor. "It was out by six inches."

"No way," I said through clenched teeth, knowing argument was a waste of time. "It was in. You're just cheating."

"I never cheat!" Grant yelled. "That ball was out—"

"Yeah, sure," I said, turning away. I was so angry my hands were trembling. It would be hard to keep control of my game, now, which is probably what he'd intended.

I took a deep breath before serving. It didn't do any good. My first serve was out by a good foot or so. I tried to put too much topspin on my second serve and it spun into the top of the net. A double fault. The first game of the set was his.

I almost felt like crying as we changed sides. It just wasn't fair. He had cheated, and there was nothing I could do about it. I closed my eyes in prayer for a moment before moving to the other side.

God, there's no way I can cheat back to make it even. I can't do that. It wouldn't be right. But I don't know what to do. If he's going to cheat like that on the really important points, how can I stop him? There is simply no way . . .

Before I'd even finished the prayer, though, I heard a very familiar voice from just behind me. "Son, was that ball really out just a minute ago?" I heard Uncle Teddy ask Evan. I whirled in confusion. What was *he* doing out here?

There was a second man standing beside my uncle, a tall, distinguished gentleman. I recognized him at once, though I'd only seen him a couple of times at the club. It was Ethan Grant, Evan's father.

"Yes, Evan. Was that ball truly out?" his father asked as well. I couldn't believe my eyes. Uncle Teddy was standing next to Evan's father casually, as if they actually knew each other. But that was impossible, I couldn't help thinking.

Evan's face was a contorted mask of rage. I could see that he was furious beyond words. "It was *out!*" he finally managed to say with a half-strangled, choking yell. "I saw it!"

His father took a step towards his son. "Evan, from where we sat, it looked good to me," he said calmly, his eyes locked on his son's. My uncle stood by his side, silent. I just watched in awe.

"It was out, I'm telling you," Evan answered beseechingly. "I won the point fair and square. I did."

I could see a fire of a very different sort smoldering within Ethan Grant. He was clearly struggling with something here. I wondered how long it had been going on.

"Evan, if you pull a stunt like that, I'm taking you off the court," his father said in a measured tone. "I mean it. I'll forfeit your match."

Evan looked stunned. His jaw dropped slightly. "But . . . but you wouldn't do that."

"Yes, I would," his father said firmly.

Evan's eyes narrowed again, the fury returning for an instant. "I can't believe you're taking *his* side," he said, jerking a thumb towards me.

"I'm taking your side, son. I really am."

"But how can you believe him over *me,*" he pleaded.

"It's not a question of who I believe," his father said, his back stiffening. "It's a question of what I saw, and of what's right and fair."

Uncle Teddy reached a hand out and placed it on Ethan Grant's shoulder, gently pulling him back towards the door. My uncle didn't say anything, though. Enough had been said already.

"But, Father, I *am* right," Evan persisted. "I am. You have to believe me."

Ethan Grant said nothing. Instead, he walked up to the court monitor briskly. "If there is another questionable call, please come get me. I'm up in the spectators' lobby," he said, looking directly at the monitor, who just nodded numbly.

Ethan Grant looked back at his son. "I meant what I said, Evan," he said grimly. "One more stunt and I'm forfeiting the match."

"But you can't do that," Evan said, still refusing to give in.

"Yes, I can, and I will," his father said, and then turned to leave the court. I couldn't believe my eyes. Uncle Teddy and Ethan Grant were conferring with each other as they walked off the court as if they'd known each other for ages. Maybe they had.

My body was tingling with the shock of what had just happened as I walked back to my position. I wondered how Evan felt. To have his own father challenge him. I couldn't imagine what it must feel like.

Actually, in a funny sort of way, it made me wish I had a father like that, someone who cared enough to reprove me, to correct me when I really messed up. I don't think Evan Grant knew just how lucky he was.

I guess it was only natural that Evan would be subdued after the encounter. His serves were somewhat lackluster, and I jumped on them right away. I broke right back to even the match on four straight points.

I could see instantly that the match was over. There was no way Evan could snap out of the coma he was in. I'd seen it happen before, although not for this kind of a reason.

But I didn't want to win this way. It wasn't right. So I suddenly called time to the monitor and walked to the net. I summoned Evan to join me there. He did so, reluctantly.

"What do *you* want?" he said morosely.

I could see that he was clearly miserable. "Look, stop worryin' about what your father said—"

"That's none of your business," he snapped back.

"Why don't you just play tennis, and just forget about everything else?"

The old Evan returned for an instant. "You can't beat me," he said, though without much enthusiasm.

"Well, prove it," I said, whacking the top of the net with my racket.

That startled him, all right. "OK, I will," he answered.

I turned and walked back to the service line, gathering balls as I went. It was crazy. I should have let him sulk. Steve would have absolutely killed me. You should never let an opponent back up when you have him down. That was the first law of tennis, or any other sport for that matter. Oh, well.

My serve was really on, now. I was sharp as a tack. I almost felt like I could pick the spot on the court I wanted the ball to go to and, presto, that's where it landed. I won my serve handily.

But Evan put up a struggle. A good one, in fact. He chased me around the court on a couple of the points before succumbing. I had clearly rekindled the old fire.

In fact, I couldn't touch his serve after we'd changed sides again. He was serving with more power than I'd seen in awhile. He even aced me on one, and won the game easily.

We fought like that—ace for ace, blast for blast, overhead for overhead, winner for winner—through the next eight games. Almost in the blink of an eye, we were all tied up, 6-6, and headed for a tiebreaker. The match, and the national title, could go either way.

It was funny, but on at least two calls during that stretch, Evan had called balls "in" that I might have called "out." I couldn't tell whether he was being generous, or just playing it safe to make sure his father didn't reemerge on the court. Either way, the match was a fair one.

I served first to start the tiebreaker. The first one to seven points won, provided you were up by at least two points. My first serve was an ace.

Evan served, then, and countered with an ace of his own. His second serve was almost as good and I could barely get my racket on it.

My two serves were both good enough to keep Evan off balance. I rushed the net both times and put winners away, one with a volley and the other with an overhead.

Evan countered with two hard serves, followed by

two driving forehands that left me completely out of position and unable to return the balls with much force. He put me away with two crosscourts.

We battled like that, neither one of us losing a single serve, point for point, shot for shot, until the twelfth point. I was beginning to wonder how long it could go on like this.

It almost ended right there. Down 5-6 on my serve, I rushed the net behind a second serve. Evan returned with a lob. I smashed it deep to his backhand side. The ball just ticked inside the line, but it was a very close call.

I could see Evan twitch for a second. He *wanted* to call it out. I could see it, clearly, on his face. All he had to do was raise his forefinger, call the ball long, and the national championship was his.

But he didn't. For whatever reason, he did the honorable thing. "In," he said miserably, raising a flat palm to indicate the ball had stayed inside the court.

My next serve was too tough to handle and I took the lead, 7-6. We changed sides. Evan didn't say anything. He just wiped some sweat off his brow and quickly moved to the other side.

His serve came in hard and deep. I lunged for the ball, not expecting to get my racket on it. Somehow, I stretched just enough to get to it. The ball drifted lazily back towards Evan's backhand, deep but not too deep. Evan took the ball at its apex, as he should, and cracked it back to my forehand side.

I ran pell-mell for the ball, almost throwing my body at it. I just barely got my racket on it again and sent a low forehand down the line to Evan, who was almost to the net by now.

He let the ball bang off his racket. The ball ticked the net on the way over, dropping on my backhand side about halfway up the court. I did a pirouette and raced like mad towards the ball, desperately trying to get to it before it bounced a second time.

I got to the ball just as it was beginning to descend a second time. I whipped my backhand just as I'd done thousands of times. The ball jumped from the racket and cleared the net by an inch. It began to angle past a somewhat startled Evan Grant.

And then it was over. Just like that. Evan couldn't get to the ball. The angle was too great. He lunged at it, giving it everything he had, but the ball shot right past him. He lay there on the ground. I threw my racket as high as I possibly could, my joy sudden and overwhelming.

I had won the national championship. Fair and square. I could hear the muffled roars and shouts of my family far, far above me, behind the window.

I looked up at my family, then, tears in my eyes. Most of them were running around the lobby, yelling at the top of their lungs. Only Chris was staring at the window, both hands held high, shouting at the top of his lungs. I had done it, after all, against the odds.

Yet, in the background, I caught a glimpse of my mother, standing next to Evan's father. While the rest of my family was going slightly crazy, she quickly embraced Ethan Grant. I was suddenly, overwhelmingly, more proud of her than I'd ever been before.

I knew, without a doubt, what was more important. Winning was great, but only for the right reasons.

I jumped across the net and offered Evan Grant, my archenemy, a helping hand. He took it, and we walked off the court together. I knew then, at that moment, that neither of us had lost.